DIANE E. TATUM

Mysteries at Kate's Bed & Breakfast, Book 1:

Surviving Renovation

by Diane E. Tatum

Scripture verses marked NIV are taken from the Holy Bible, New International Version, copyright 1973, 1978, 1984, 2011 by Biblica, Inc. Used by permission of Zondervan Publishing House. All rights reserved.

This novel is a work of fiction. It is placed in a real town and reference to some places in Adams, Springfield, and to the Bell Witch are accurate. Other names, descriptions, entities, and incidents included in the story are products of the author's imagination.

1. Fiction/Christian/Romantic Suspense/Mystery
2. Fiction/Christian/Romance/Suspense
3. Cozy Mystery
4. Cozy Mystery (book)

ISBN-13: 978-1-959788-47-8

moments that made me gasp! I am glad they finally fixed the house up and opened her bed and breakfast. Have you ever been in a house that resembled this one? Lots of different rooms and areas to get lost in. Adds to the mystery. Also, glad she got a dog. That did help save her! Thanks for letting me be a part of your new book!

Katherine Hasty

Dedicated to my one and only, my husband, Ken,
to my family who support, and
to my dear friends who cheer me on in this writing
endeavor.
May all your mysteries be harmless and may all
your loves forever be strong.

"For I know the plans I have for you," declares the LORD,
"plans to prosper you and not to harm you,
plans to give you hope and a future.

Jeremiah 29:11

But let all who take refuge in you be glad;
let them ever sing for joy.
Spread your protection over them,
that those who love your name may rejoice in you.
12 Surely, LORD, you bless the righteous;
you surround them with your favor as with a shield.
Psalm 5:11-12 NIV

Chapter 1

Moving to Adams …

Kate exhaled a breath of tension she didn't even realize she was holding as she drove into the small town of Adams, Tennessee. She had said good-bye to her modern apartment in Nashville. Everything she wanted to keep in her life was in the trunk, the back seat of her car, and a storage rental. While it wasn't a long way from Nashville, the change in her life was complete. Even her boyfriend Brian had ended their relationship. saying the less than one hour drive was too far to travel while he pursued his own dreams as a musician in Music City, USA.

When Great-Aunt Katharine died, the lawyer had contacted Kate about the will.

"To my dear niece, Kate Winslow, I leave the entirety of my estate including the family home at Four-Fifteen Spring Street, Adams, Tennessee."

Kate had visited her Great-Aunt Katharine as a child every summer until she was ten and remembered a place of wonder: creaky stairs with green oriental carpet held down at the risers with heavy brass rods, wavy rainbow window glass, a mysterious attic full of treasures and antique furniture, a fabulous library in the turret, and a porch that wrapped around the house. The porch swing was her favorite place in the summer to enjoy the evening breezes and fireflies.

Too many summers had passed since she'd visited her aunt in that lovely Victorian home. It had been her grandmother's home and her great-grandmother's home before that. When her aunt had become ill, she'd moved from her wonderful three-story home to a one-story care facility, lingering for so many years at the edge of a mysterious reality.

Siri broke into her thoughts. "Turn right onto Church Street in 0.4 miles." She passed the Red River Baptist Church, established in 1791.

"Turn right onto Highway 41."

When she reached the stop sign at the US Post Office, Kate turned into the small-town world of Adams. All the houses were southern homes in various states of decay. Some had been renovated. Some had been replaced; some had been allowed to fall in.

Highway 41 split the town. Traffic with no intent to stop before the Kentucky border seven miles away zipped by. City Hall was housed in the old Bell High School with a museum and replica soda shoppe inside.

"Turn left onto Keysburg." A sign at the intersection announced the Historic Bell Witch Cave nearby.

"In 0.3 miles, turn left on Spring Street." Kate made the turn.

Half a block from Keysburg, Siri GPS announced, "You have arrived at your destination."

Kate did a double take. This was not the grand house she remembered as a child. Aunt Katharine's home was now an old, destitute Victorian house. The windows were boarded up. The gravel driveway to the alley had large, stubborn-looking weeds growing in it. The color was no longer the teal she remembered, but a sad gray. She drove her car over the bumpy drive to the garage that faced the alley shared by all the other houses on that block.

"Siri, put gravel and yardwork on the TO DO List."

The garage had carriage house style doors, sporting a multi-colored mural of spray paint graffiti. It included an inspired version of the town's most famous character, Kate Batts's Witch, also known as the Bell Witch.

"Siri, add paint the garage door on the TO DO List."

Kate climbed out of her royal blue Fusion and pulled open the wooden doors. She moved a few collapsed stacks of newspapers and plastic flowerpots to the sides in order to make room for her car. Paint cans, spider webs, clay pots, and other debris were piled on top of more clutter.

"Siri, add declutter garage to the TO DO List."

She pulled the car in and closed the alley garage door. The door from the garage led into the backyard, the Secret Garden of her childhood. Now it was covered in dead overgrowth. The back of the house was just as bleak as the front.

"Oh, Siri, what have I done?"

Siri replied, "I don't know that answer," to which Kate just sighed.

Kate used her key to enter the back of the house into the large kitchen. The boards on the windows blocked the natural light. She wandered through the house, at once familiar, yet totally strange, covered in sheets and dust.

"Siri, I'm going to need a motel for tonight."

She waited on the front porch swing, which also needed a fresh coat of paint, for the utility turn-on services to arrive, resulting in the miracles of water, electricity, and natural gas. Internet and cable TV could wait for now.

Kate's first stop the next morning after the motel breakfast was the town hardware store.

The bell jangled as she opened the door.

"Good morning. What can I do you for?" The man who perched on a stool behind the counter was bursting at the seams of his overalls. His smile just as wide.

"Hi, I'm Kate Winslow. I just inherited my Aunt Katharine's house on Spring Street." She offered her hand and then thought better of it. *I don't know who this is! However, it would be rude to withdraw it now.*

The man grabbed her hand and shook it with gusto. "Little Katie? I remember you from ages ago. I'm Uncle Porter. Not really your uncle, but that's what you called me when you came to visit all those years ago."

Kate tried to dredge up a memory of him but failed. "Wow. That's been fifteen years ago I'm afraid."

"Sorry Kathy has entered glory. Seems once folks go to a care facility, no one remembers to tell the neighbors and friends from their life before dementia. I sure have missed Kathy. She was a dear friend of mine."

"I'm sorry. The obit was supposed to run in the local paper."

"Water under the bridge now. How can I help?"

"I want to open the old house and make it into a bed and breakfast. I need a handyman to help me. Know anybody reliable?"

Porter twisted his mouth and stroked his face. "He's pretty busy, but I'll check with Billy. If he can't help you, I'll recommend someone else." He took a card from a holder on the counter. "Here's his information. Can I give him your number?"

"Of course." Kate dug around in her purse until she found an old business card and a pen. She wrote her cell phone number on the back. "Here's my number. Everything else is history." She scratched out her old business info then added 415 Spring Street. "I can use his help right away."

"I'll let him know as soon as I see him." Porter tapped the card on the counter. "You know, Adams ain't a bustling city like Nashville."

Kate smiled. "I know. But everyone in Nashville has to escape to somewhere. Small town rural Tennessee is as good a place as any, I figure."

"Good luck in your venture. Billy will be glad to see you again."

"Thanks. I should probably look around. I'll need some hardware stuff to make a dent in the rust, dust, and drop cloths." Kate turned away from him, grabbed a basket, and began choosing stuff from the shelves: trash bags, paint brushes, cleaning supplies, a hammer, wrought iron decorative house numbers, and a gallon of teal-gray paint, Number 1526 Victorian Seaside, to cover the graffiti on the alley garage door. *Billy? Is that the boy I used to pal around with when I was here as a kid?*

Porter had disappeared by the time she brought her mishmash of hardware supplies to the counter. She dinged the bell and hoped that was why it was there.

A young man appeared from the shelves of clutter behind the counter. His dark hair was short but shaggy. His dark brown eyes took in hers. "How can I help, ma'am?"

"First, don't call me ma'am. I'm not my mom."

The man smiled. His teeth weren't braces-straight nor model perfect, but his smile raced to her heart. "Is there something else you'd like me to call you? After all, you are the new girl in town."

"Call me Kate." She ran her hand through her long auburn hair. "I want to buy all this."

"Big project, Kate?"

"Opening the house at Four-Fifteen Spring. I just inherited it from my Aunt Katharine."

"That's been empty a long time."

Kate nodded. She'd already given this stranger way too much information.

He nodded, as though understanding why she'd pulled back, and rang up all the items. "One hundred fifty dollars and forty-five cents, Kate."

She handed him her credit card. *The first of much more.* She sighed.

The man ran her card then handed it back to her. "Nice to meet you, Kate Winslow."

"I didn't get your name." Kate held her breath. *He is so lovely.*

"Will Bell, no relation."

Kate stared at him. "No relation?"

"Yeah, to the Bell Witch. No relation to the Bell family of Adams folklore."

Kate smiled. "Nice to meet you, Will Bell, no relation."

"See you around, Katie."

The bell on the door jangled as she departed. Katie. She'd spent half of her life, since middle school, trying to rid herself of that nickname, so she'd be taken seriously in her profession. But something about Will saying it made it seem okay. After all, she wasn't in Nashville anymore.

Chapter 2

Making a place to sleep …

After her trip to the hardware store, Kate arrived at the house on Spring Street about nine o'clock. The sun accentuated the house's extreme neglect. Flaking paint, boards on the windows, a loose shutter banging in the breeze, graffiti referencing the Bell Witch again. Kate's rose-colored glasses had been removed. Since she hoped to stop spending her money on the motel, her priority was to make the house livable, at least for just herself.

She took the weedy gravel drive to the back, then struggled with the wooden garage doors that opened like French doors. After parking, she deposited her hardware purchases on the rickety workbench to retrieve as she had need of them. For now, she needed to make coffee and find a bedroom she could sleep in.

When Kate opened the back door to the kitchen, the house seemed to welcome her. Her memories of summers in Adams were full of joy. She set up the coffeepot and started it. While the coffee dripped, she wandered into the living room and pulled dust covers off the furniture and the piano. Then she climbed the stairs with the threadbare green oriental carpet. The heavy brass riser bars still held down the carpet runner at the base of each step, but the carpet needed to be replaced. "Siri, add tune piano and replace stair carpet to the TO DO list."

The stairs creaked as ever before. Only as an adult, she hoped they'd hold her. Ending up in the root cellar at the end of a three-story drop was not on her bucket list. She could imagine her aunt and mom on either side of her as she climbed those complaining stairs. She felt their love, but the thought brought tears to her eyes.

At the top of the first set of stairs was the master bedroom. As she entered, she smelled a whiff of Katharine's signature perfume. Chanel No.5. Kate could hear her mother singing "Love Potion Number Nine." She laughed at that memory. The two of them had been best friends besides being niece and aunt.

"Hello, Aunt Katharine. Is this room okay for me?"

Every generation in her family had named the oldest daughter some variation of Katharine all the way back to the early 1800s. Her great-grandmother was Katerina, her great-aunt was Katharine, her mother was Katelyn.

Kate wedged open the window with great effort. Was every window stuck closed with paint? She shoved on the boards covering it. One broke free, but before she could grab it, it clattered down the porch roof and slammed onto the sidewalk.

"Hey! Be careful up there!" A deep male voice shouted up at her. He stepped out into the sunshine.

Will Bell, no relation. *Why did he seem so familiar?*

"Sorry, Will. I was just trying to make at least one

of these rooms usable for me while I make the rest of the place presentable."

He shaded his eyes. "I rang the bell. Didn't you hear it?"

"No. I guess that's something else to repair. I'll be right down."

Kate left the other boards and hurried down the stairs, each footfall echoing as she went. When she got to the bottom of the staircase, she struggled with the front door lock before opening it to him.

"A shot of WD-40 would fix that latch."

Kate nodded. "Come in. The coffee's hot if you'd like some."

"That sounds great." Will followed her to the kitchen. "Do you have any idea where you'd like me to begin?"

"What do you mean?" She poured the coffee in a mug she'd washed that morning and handed it to him. "Some guy named Billy Bob is coming by to do the handyman stuff."

Will pointed to his embroidered hardware shirt. "Billy Bell, at your service."

Kate pursed her lips. "Sorry, you told me you were Will. Guess I'm not the only one trying to get rid of their childhood nickname, huh?"

"You don't like Katie? I think it suits you. And that's probably what they'll call you in town. Your aunt was Kathy. I know she always said she was Katharine, but it didn't matter." He sipped the black coffee. "We're a rural Tennessee town. We don't put on airs here."

"But you still introduced yourself to me as Will." Kate crossed her arms and leaned back against the counter.

"Doesn't mean I don't want to get rid of Billy Bob Bell. Sounds like a twisted fairy tale to me." He set down the mug and laid a leather portfolio on the counter. He pulled out a pen and opened the portfolio to a legal pad. "What things do you need done, Katie?"

She shuddered for his benefit, but the way he said her name in his sonorous deep voice made her nickname sound regal, beloved. He could call her Katie anytime he wanted. She could feel the blush starting at the roots of her hair. Too soon to fall in love with anyone.

"I'd like to be able to sleep in the master bedroom soon, so I'm not paying for the motel room. And I'd like the kitchen to be functional to start."

He scribbled on his legal pad and grabbed a barstool, dragged it over to the counter, and perched on it. "I can easily pull the boards from the windows and check the appliances in here. Do you want to do any updates as we go? Or is this bare bones for now?"

Kate thought of her savings and the inheritances from her mom, dad, and aunt. It wasn't a lot, but she hoped it was enough to make this place a thriving business. "I guess it depends on how much work she needs."

Will clicked his pen three times. "What if, after I pop the boards off the windows, I spend some time looking 'her' over. I'll make a list of things that must be done as well as a list of things that could be done easily and with not too much expense. Are all the utilities on?"

"I had them turned on yesterday. How can I help?" Kate didn't intend to eat bonbons while Will hammered all over the house. It was her house after all.

"Start in the kitchen. Open drawers, Run the water. Make sure everything works, including the electrical outlets, refrigerator, oven, and stove top. Wipe down everything. Mop the floor. Then hit the master bedroom. Uncover the furniture in there. Vacuum. Check the floors and walls for watermarks and flaws. WD-40 is the answer to opening the windows." Will made a list as he spoke. "We can assemble back in the kitchen then go out for a bite at the diner and run some numbers. Sound okay?"

Kate saw dollar signs with every word he spoke, but she knew that's where her money was going. Plus, what she could do, she didn't have to pay him to do. She nodded. "Sounds like a plan, Billy Bob Bell."

Will closed the portfolio. "My middle name is not Robert or Bob. It's Chadwick, my mom's maiden name."

Kate traced the embossed letters on the worn portfolio, WCB. "Billy Chad doesn't have the same ring to it."

"Praise God." He looked heavenward and nodded. "Small favors. We don't get to pick our names, family, or burdens to bear. I'll get started on those boards and try not to hit any unsuspecting visitors." He picked up a can of WD-40 and headed upstairs.

Kate wanted to protest that she expected no such person, but then she hadn't really expected Will either. Her heart skipped a beat when he smiled. *Was he her Billy from childhood?* After Brian, a stab of pain in her heart told her it was way too soon to play romantic games … yet.

She ran a sink of hot water. Thank goodness, it was

hot. She turned on the overhead light and wiped down all the surfaces. The stove gas came on, flames flickered to life on each burner, and the oven lit. It looked relatively new, as did the refrigerator. That was a blessing. However, there was no dishwasher. Kate emptied each cabinet and washed each dirty dish, utensil, pan, and casserole dish.

She found a stiff, old rope mop in the cupboard and a bucket along with a nearly empty bottle of pine cleaner in the cobwebby metal bucket. She rinsed out the dead bugs and webbing. When a bug of some kind ran out from under the rim and across her hand, the old metal bucket went flying across the floor, clanging and dinging while splashing water across the black and white tile floor. Kate covered her mouth with her hand, trying not to scream.

Will ran into the kitchen and slipped on one of the puddles the bucket had left behind. He lost his balance and ended up flat on his back.

"Are you okay?" Kate's voice rose an octave. "You're not hurt, are you?" She hurried to his side to help him up. She slipped in the water and ended up beside him on the floor.

The multi-legged creature crawled across her jeans. She shrieked and swiped at it, trying not to freak out.

"Is that what this is about?" Will propped himself up on his elbow. "We call that a centipede."

"It has so many legs!" Kate was bordering on hysteria as the critter ran under the refrigerator. "It could come back out!"

Will started laughing, and he seemed unable to stop. Kate got up from the floor and grabbed the bucket, carefully inspecting the inside and outside. That action sent Will into new peals of laughter.

"You are not helping!" Kate's voice shrieked to a new high. "I don't care what you call it. It's disgusting." She folded her arms over her chest.

Will sat up, fighting back tears and further guffaws. "They have a right to live like anything else. Remember, you are the one invading his space, not the other way 'round." Will finally stood up.

"If you wanted to help, you'd move the refrigerator and kill it."

Will touched her elbow. "You really want the critter dead? He's probably already slipped into the wall space."

Kate shuddered. "Thanks for that image in my head."

"Well, I'll leave you to it." Will went back to the regular cadence of his hammer, removing the boards from the front of the house.

"Siri, add insecticide, window cleaner, floor cleaner, a bucket, and a new mop to the shopping list."

Will found Katie in the master bedroom vacuuming and dusting at noon. The room had the smell of a musty perfume. The ancient vacuum she'd found somewhere was gasping for life. She'd need a new one to care for this old place. He had to wonder if it was worth the work and money to fix it back up. Kathy probably hadn't been able to care for it for a while before she went to the assisted care home. The dust under the dust covers attested to that.

Will went in and tapped her on the shoulder. "Ready for lunch?"

Katie jumped a foot and grabbed her chest. Then she hit him. "Don't ever do that again, to anyone, at any time, but especially not in a room that still smells so much like her."

Will laughed. She hit him again.

"Sorry, I just wanted to know if you're ready to knock off for lunch and go over my appraisal of the situation."

Katie closed her beautiful brown eyes and breathed slowly. "Lunch sounds great. I can pay since you're on my time."

"Let's take my truck."

Will was headed down the stairs when he heard her say, "Siri, add a vacuum to the retrieve list."

He grinned. She was something different than any other girl in town. And the project would take a while, maybe long enough for them to get to know each other again. And no, she'd not be paying for lunch. It was a business expense as well as an investment in getting to know Katie.

Chapter 3

Getting to know you …

Will opened the door to his beat-up red truck for her. Katie's auburn hair was mussed, with strands of red hanging out of her ponytail, and she had a smudge on her cheek. But somehow, she looked all the better for it. Unspoiled. Sweet in an unpretentious way in her jeans and tee shirt. Looking more like a country gal than a city girl.

He closed the door and headed to the driver's side. Katie was a cute thing. After his last relationship, though, he knew to stay clear until he was sure of any girl. Had Katie remembered how long they'd known each other?

Katie flipped down the sunshade and checked the mirror. "Why'd you let me leave the house looking a fright?" She took out the ponytail and her hair tumbled down to her shoulders. Katie ran her fingers through it and re-pulled it into the elastic band. Then she rubbed the smudge on her cheek. "The town will think I'm unkempt."

"Nah, you look fine. Adams is used to hard-working people. They don't pay much attention to a little bit of dirt." Will started the truck and shifted into drive. The gears ground as the truck left the curb.

"Your truck is about as well off as my house." Katie laughed. "What does that say about us?"

"We care about what we have, we hold onto what we have a long time, and we take care of it as best we can." He drove the couple of blocks to the diner and pulled into a spot in front. Will hopped out and hurried around to her side. He opened the door and swept his arm before her. "My fair lady."

Katie laughed again, like sparkling water in the spring that ran through Adams. Fresh, clean, bubbly. She hopped out of the truck and headed to the diner's door.

The smell of hot grease assaulted the senses. Hamburger, bacon, cheese, and fries.

"Nothing changes in small towns." Katie slid into a booth and grabbed a menu. "I always get the breakfast even at lunch. Eggs, hash browns scattered, smothered, covered. Coffee."

"Sounds great to me. Dana, two breakfast specials, scattered, smothered, covered. Two coffees. I'm hungry!"

The waitress nodded and brought over the coffeepot and a pair of mugs.

"Who you got here, Billy?" Dana poured the coffee.

"I'm Kate Winslow. My aunt was Katharine Avery. I'm renovating her house on Spring Street."

Dana leaned back against the counter, revealing impending motherhood. "We always thought that house was haunted, especially after Miss Kathy moved away."

"When are you due?" Katie slapped her hand over

her mouth and a hot blush surged into her face.

"It's okay, Katie. It's not like it's not noticeable. My little boy is due in about a month. Not soon enough, but also way too soon. I'll go check on your order."

When they finished eating and Dana took the plates, Kate motioned to Will. "Bring out the portfolio. Show me the notes you've made."

Will opened it and showed her the numbers. "Keep in mind, you don't have to do all these fixes immediately."

"Goodness. It would take a fortune to make the place livable much less to make a business of it." Kate buried her face in her hands. "What should I do?"

"What if I do the work *pro bono*?" Will touched her arm.

"I can't let you do that." Kate pulled away from him. "I have to pay you if you do the work."

"What if you give me a share in the house? We work together to fix it up, we share the profits of the business. When it's paid off, it's done."

Kate looked at him. His eyes were clear. *Can I trust him? I just met grown up Will this morning.* She looked at his figures. She'd never be able to pay him from her savings. Would a bank lend her the money? If she wanted to fix the house, she'd have to find another way.

"Okay, but I'm paying you back every penny. I won't take advantage of your goodness." Kate took his portfolio and his pen. She scrawled across the bottom of the page. "IOU. In exchange for the labor to repair 415

Spring Street, I guarantee a share of the proceeds of the business to repay said labor until it is reimbursed." Then she signed her name.

Will took back the portfolio. "Fair enough. I'll get Dad's lawyer to draw up a simple contract."

"Are you sure, Will? You barely know me."

"Not a problem, Katie. I can invest in you and in Adams." Will smiled at her. "I can do the work, you can buy the materials, we can make the business work, Besides, we've known each other a long time."

"So, you do remember me from those long-ago summers?"

"How could I ever forget the girl who stole my heart?"

Heat rushed up her neck into her face. *Stole his heart?* Feeling flustered, Kate stuck out her hand and nodded. "It's a deal."

A teenage girl came up to the table. "Are you the lady who's waking up the house on Spring Street?" Another girl and a boy joined her.

"Yes, I am. It was my Aunt Katharine's." Kate smiled at her.

"Is it true your name is Kate?" The girl backed a step away from the table.

"It is. I was named after my great-aunt and mom."

"I'm telling you, she's the Witch. The Bell Witch come back to the house to haunt us." The younger girl grabbed the boy's hand.

The boy backed farther away.

The three looked back and forth among themselves, then they shrieked and ran from the diner.

"Are they kidding, or do they really believe that?" Kate sat back in the booth. "Have you seen the garage door? Someone painted graffiti of the Bell Witch on my garage door. Do they really believe what they're saying?"

Will came over to the other side of the booth and sat beside her. "I wouldn't worry, Katie. They're just kids with crazy ideas. It's your aunt's house, nothing more than that. Let's go see if we can knock some of these projects off our list."

"I need to pick up more cleaning supplies."

"Luckily my dad's hardware store is right next door." He scooted over to let her out. He also picked up the check.

"Hey, I was going to get that." Kate flipped her ponytail.

"Too late. I got it." Will pulled his wallet from his jeans.

Kate cleared her throat. "I'll go ahead and get those supplies then."

The hardware store was indeed next door to the diner. The bell on the door jangled as Kate pushed it open.

Will is my hero, swooping in to solve my problems.

She grabbed a cart for all the things she needed now: a new broom, bucket and mop, window cleaner and paper towels, more trash bags, a basic set of screwdrivers, and a box of nails.

Will's dad waited on her. "How's the house?"

"Needs more work than I thought it would. Will's kind enough to help." Kate put the stuff from her cart on the counter. "So, you're Will's dad, the man I called

Uncle Porter?"

He nodded. "You finally remember us? Billy's a hard worker with a heart of gold. Smart too. Just graduated with an engineering degree from Tennessee Tech." Uncle Porter rang each item as she took it out of the cart.

Kate's credit card took another hit. She hurried to Will's truck with her supplies where he was chewing on a toothpick with his cap bill pulled down over his handsome face. *And oh yes, he is pleasant to look at.* Now they were in business together. She hadn't even remembered he existed that morning.

"I'm back, Will. I guess we'd best get at it."

He raised his bill and gazed on her. Will's dark brown eyes twinkled in the noon sun. Kate could feel the blush from her toes. *Oh yes, he was quite nice to look at.*

"Yes, partner." Will opened her door then placed her goods in the back of the truck. "Let's go." He returned and closed her door.

After the vacuum finally died, Kate decided to work in the garage.

She used the trash bags to gather most of the clutter. Aunt Katharine saved everything. Aluminum pie pans, flowerpots, hanging plastic planters, even Styrofoam meat trays. In addition, she had near empty paint cans from twenty years or more ago. Unfortunately, not garbage bag stuff. She found a rusted toolbox with neglected tools. Dirty rag and greasy towels were piled into an old trash can. Once all the trash had filled the can, Kate began removing the packaging from all the new paint supplies. Finally, she pulled open her new can of Number 1526 Victorian Seaside paint and poured it into her tray.

She dragged the ladder out of the garage.

"Mew!" A black kitten curled around Kate's ankles, startling her and knocking the ladder into the driveway. Kitty jumped back then crawled back to Kate.

"Kitty, what are you doing? A good thing it wasn't the paint, or you'd be a teal-gray kitty instead of a black kitty." She squatted down and scratched the cat's head. "You're a sweetie, but I can't take in a kitten. Pretty sure the Department of Health would not look kindly on a cat in the bed & breakfast, climbing all over the place."

She picked up the old, dilapidated ladder. Rickety and dangerous. She placed it beside the trash bin for the next pickup.

"Siri, add a ladder to the TO DO list."

Kate sighed. The black kitten hopped back and forth, biting at Kate's exposed toes in her sandals. "Stop that. Go home. Scat!"

The kitten hissed and sulked while walking down the alley.

"I'm sure you belong to someone who is missing you." Kate placed the tray on the concrete wall separating her drive from her neighbor's. She rolled the first paint over the graffiti of the Bell Witch.

Will knocked down the last of the boards from the windows. It clattered to the sidewalk that went around the house to the garden. He climbed down his ladder and closed the grimy window. *Didn't Kate buy window cleaner and paper towels?* He could clean some windows for her. He still had an hour or two. He checked in each of the bedrooms, but she wasn't there. The master bedroom had the vacuum in the center of the room, abandoned. *Is she okay?*

Will checked the parlor, the great room, and the dining room as he hurried down to the kitchen. She wasn't in the kitchen either. He headed out the back door into the garden.

"Katie? Where are you? Are you okay?" He hurried to the garage.

Will entered the pitch-black garage. He flipped on the light. She'd been here. The place had been emptied except for an open can of paint. He tamped the lid closed.

"Katie?" Will pushed open the carriage house style garage door.

"Wait! No! Oh no!"

The clatter of a wooden ladder and a thud hurried Will to the other side of the door.

The concrete was awash in Victorian Seaside. A wooden ladder was in pieces. Katie lay on the driveway, her left arm bent at an odd angle.

"Oh, Katie, I'm so sorry." Will squatted down beside her. "Is your arm broken?"

"Most probably." She shuddered in pain.

He pulled his plaid shirt off, revealing his white tee shirt. He helped her up and used his shirt to make a sling.

"I'll go get the truck, and we'll take a trip to the medical center in Springfield."

25

Chapter 4

The alliance …

It was dark as Kate left the hospital with a cast on her arm in a real sling. Will helped her into his truck.

"I am so sorry, Katie. I never wanted to hurt you." Will helped her put on her seatbelt. "Where are you sleeping tonight?"

"My stuff is still at the motel. I didn't know how much I'd get done. I had hoped to move in tomorrow." Kate rubbed her forehead. "But I can't do anything with one arm."

After Will closed the door, he went around to the driver's side and climbed in. He pulled away from the medical center. "You should not have been on that ladder."

"I just needed to reach the witch's hat to finish covering her, so I used the old ladder I had put out for trash pickup." Kate didn't need any "told you so's" right now. "It didn't help that someone knocked me over. I could have sworn it was you."

"Maybe it was the Bell Witch." Will gave a short laugh.

"I did have an encounter with a black kitten on the

driveway."

"I'm going to help you." Will's words were quiet but forceful. "Remember, we're partners in the house. Let me help."

"I need to sleep now. My arm hurts. I can pay you for your labor for today. I'm going to have to just go slower than I'd hoped. We can talk tomorrow."

Will shook his head. "Don't make any big decisions tonight when you're in pain and taking pain meds." He drove to the motel and dropped her off.

Kate let herself into her motel room and waved as Will pulled out. She closed her door and leaned against it. *Maybe I should have stayed in Nashville. I had a job, a nice place to live, and Brian.*

Loneliness, pain, and heartache – the trifecta. *Why I ever thought I could do this, I have no idea.* She collapsed on the bed, her whole body aching as well as her arm from housework instead of her desk job on Music Row. *Then there was Will.* She fell asleep in her clothes. She probably couldn't have changed out of them by herself anyway with only one arm.

Will's black lab greeted him heartily at the door as he entered his parents' home. Their Black Forest cuckoo clock sounded nine times. "Hey, boy. How're you doing, Walker? Good boy." The dog headed back to the den with a backward glance, expecting him to follow.

Any day that ended at the hospital was a bad day. He blushed thinking about how he'd caused her injury. What was he going to do to help her tomorrow?

"Billy? That you, son?" Dad called from the den where the TV blared.

Will sighed and turned around to see his parents.

"It's me. I just dropped Katie at her motel after taking her to the hospital for a broken arm." He perched on the end of the couch next to his mom. "She fell off a rickety ladder." He shook his head, feeling disappointed at himself.

"Billy, why you so down on yourself?" Mom patted his hand.

"I caused it. She was painting the garage door, and I opened it from inside the garage."

"Aw, sweet baby, that ain't your fault." Mom stood. "Have you eaten?"

Will shook his head. "Just vending machine snacks. It took forever to get her treated." He ran his hands through his hair. "I just feel like an idiot. She's such a dreamer. Now she's hurt and depressed."

His mom wrapped her arms around him.

"Aw, Maddy, don't baby the boy. He's a grown man. He's got to step up and take responsibility for his actions, the good and the bad." Dad threw a wadded napkin at him.

"Don't pick on the boy, Porter." Mom hugged him. "Is someone there to help her undress tonight? Who's going to help her in the morning?"

Dad continued the interrogation. "Where's her car? You pickin' her up tomorrow?"

Will had nothing to say. He hadn't thought of any of those things.

Maddy patted Will's knee. "Don't worry, son. Take me over there in the morning. I'll help her. I want to meet Kathy's niece, all grown up. Let me get you a bowl of mint chocolate chip.”

Once his mom had left the room, Will dropped into a recliner and leaned it back.

“Son, what is it about this girl that’s got you so wound up? You just met her today after all these years, y’know?” Dad cut off the TV.

“She hasn’t got enough money to do all the repairs I’d need to do to fix it up as a bed and breakfast. So, I agreed to donate my labor for a share in the business.”

Dad’s eyebrows rose. “Are you crazy? Doing labor for a business that won’t be operating for a while? Might not even happen. How bad off is the house?”

“The bones are good. Doesn’t appear to have termite damage. Appliances need updating, but they work for now. Paint, minor repairs, floor refinishing, carpet on the stairs needs replacing. May see more as we dig into it.” Will crossed his arms behind his head. “I know what I’m doing, Dad. I need this project while I wait for that dream structural engineer job to use my diploma from Tech. No one’s really hiring right now.”

“There’s the hardware store. Eventually, I thought you’d take it over.”

Mom returned with three bowls of ice cream balancing in her hands. She stopped at his dad who took one allowing her to hold on to the other bowls. She handed one to Will then returned to her spot on the couch with the third.

“That’s your dream, Dad.” He spooned the green ice cream flecked with chocolate shavings into his mouth. “Mm. That hits the spot. Thank you.”

“Who’s going to take it over then? Joe’s farming that acreage behind the house.”

“Dad, we’ve had this fight before. I just can’t take

it over."

Silence pervaded the den as the Bell family, no relation, ate their ice cream.

Kate woke to a gentle rap on the door of her motel room. She was lying right where she'd lay down. She checked her phone. 7:00.

"Just a minute!" She rolled onto her good arm and shoved herself upright. "Sleeping in my clothes is a bad sign." Her arm throbbed.

Kate opened the door with the chain on it to reveal the kind face of a plump woman. "Hi, what can I do for you?"

"I'm Madeline Bell, no relation, Billy's mom. I heard you might have trouble dressing today, so Billy brought me by to see if I can help you."

Kate saw Will's truck in the lot. He was resting against it like he had yesterday, ball cap pulled down, arms crossed over his chest.

"Thank you. I probably do need some help." Kate unchained the door and let Will's mom in. "I guess I slept in my clothes."

Madeline Bell entered carrying a big tote bag. "This motel is so dingy. How can you bear it, Katie?"

"It's just until I can sleep at the house."

"Is that so?" She frowned and reached into her bag and withdrew a yellow box of plastic wrap. "We can wrap up that cast, so you can shower."

Twenty minutes later, Kate had showered and put on fresh clothing with Madeline's help.

Madeline brushed her hair for her. "You got the prettiest red hair, Katie. Your aunt Kathy had hair like this when she was a younger woman. We've missed her." She gathered Kate's auburn locks, put them in a ponytail, then wrapped it all into a messy bun. "There. Ready for whatever the day brings."

Kate slipped on her sandals, which Madeline secured for her.

"I'm thinking you should move out of this place into the guest room at Chez Bell." She put her hands on her hips. "You know that house needs more work before you can sleep there, especially with this broken arm."

"I couldn't do that. You don't even know me, Mrs. Bell."

"Call me Madeline or Maddy. I insist. I've known you since you were born, Katie. You played at my house with Will near every summer until your Mama passed. Let's gather up all your stuff. Will can put it in the truck while you check out. Then you're coming with us to the diner for coffee and such." She held up her hand. "I'm not takin' no for an answer, Katie Winslow."

Kate sighed. "Okay."

Maddy opened the motel door and called to Will. "Come here and help us."

Kate threw stuff into the suitcase. She checked the bathroom, bureau drawers, and surfaces for anything she might have forgotten.

Will entered the room. "Good morning, partner. How's the arm this morning?"

His deep voice and presence took her breath away. "It hurts. I need to take some pain meds, but I don't want to do that on an empty stomach."

"Gotcha. Let's get your stuff in the truck and go on to the diner." Will took over zipping Kate's suitcase.

Madeline grabbed her tote bag and plastic wrap, leaving Kate and Will in the motel room.

Kate picked up her purse. "I'll walk down to the lobby and check out. Your mom invited me to use her guest room for a bit."

"That sounds like something my mom would devise." He laughed. "She picks up strays, like kittens, puppies, and women, it seems."

Kate wasn't sure how to respond to that. "I must look a fright to be considered a stray. I was an almost important Music Row executive, you know."

"No, you look just..." He paused for a second and looked her up and down. "… fine, Katie girl. You look gorgeous." He grabbed the handle of her suitcase and headed out the door. "This all you got?"

"The rest is stowed in my car at the house and at a storage facility in Nashville."

"Let me help you unpack your car today. There's room in the garage since you threw out all the junk in it. I'm hungry. Let's get a move on."

Kate laughed despite the pain. "Let's do this." She headed out to the sidewalk in the cool damp air, motel key in hand. Once the haze burned off, it was going to be a scorcher.

Will closed the door and dragged her wheeled suitcase across the parking lot to his truck where Maddy was waiting.

Kate walked down to the lobby and checked out. As she was stuffing the bill into her purse, she noticed the display of tourist advertisements for things to see in the area. A pamphlet labeled "The Legend of the Bell Witch" caught her attention. She picked it up, but before she could read it, Will pulled his truck up to the lobby door. She stuffed it into her purse too.

When she reached the truck cab, Will opened the door, but Maddy slid out and allowed Kate to sit in between the two of them.

"I'm starved, ladies. Let's eat." Will closed the passenger door and hurried around to the driver's side. When he slid in, his broad shoulders touched hers. His mom's touched hers on the other side. *Cozy. Was this some kind of match-maker thing by Maddy?*

Chapter 5

Unusual occurrences begin …

Breakfast at the diner was as good as breakfast at lunch had been. Kate took her pain medication, even though she was afraid she'd be too groggy to work at the house. Nevertheless, she'd soldier on.

Leaving there, Will soon pulled up in front of a historic-looking house.

Mrs. Bell hopped out of the truck cab, and Kate scooted over to the passenger's seat. Will took Kate's luggage into the house. After some trial and error, Kate managed to put on the seat belt with one hand.

Do I remember being here? Perhaps.

Will startled her when he climbed in. "All set? Are you feeling okay to go to the house today?" Will reached over and touched her cast. "You can just stay here if you need to. I can work at the store."

"Do you need the day to work with your dad?" Kate wanted to determine his motive for suggesting it. "I can work at the house by myself. The windows won't clean themselves. I can do the insides without hurting my arm. Great-aunt Katharine's old vacuum died, so I can't do that until I go to Nashville get my vacuum from my storage unit."

"If you're sure, I'll take you over." Will started the truck and threw it into gear. "Let me know when you're ready to come back to the house. Call my phone, so you have my number."

He told her the number as he drove out Spring Street and turned down the alley. His phone rang until Kate hung up.

"I need to run an errand for my dad this morning. Let me see you safely into the house." He pulled into the paint-splattered drive.

Kate gasped. The picture of the Bell Witch had reappeared through the paint. "How did that happen? I covered it all except the witch's hat."

Will jumped out of the truck and ran over to the carriage style doors. Kate struggled with the seat belt and door. Once free, she followed him to the graffiti. Sure enough, it was on top of the paint Kate had used to cover it.

"It's probably nothing. The paint on the graffiti bled through. Or your vandals came back last night." Will touched the paint. "Seems dry. I'll pick up some primer to cover the graffiti. Then I'll paint over it later with your house paint."

"Victorian Seaside, if you need more. Guess I need a new ladder too." Kate sighed. The task of rescuing this old house was bigger than Kate had imagined. She was reliant on Will's good graces.

"I'll bring mine when I come back with the primer." Will put a hand on her good shoulder. "Don't worry. Every project starts like this. We never know the path until we start down it."

"Yea, though I walk through the valley of the

shadow of death ..." Kate rolled her eyes.

"No, He maketh me to lie down in green pastures: he leadeth me beside the still waters." Will slid his hand down her arm and took her hand. "The Lord knows the path and its end. Our job is to walk where He leads us. You're here for a reason, Katie Winslow. The path may seem difficult, but you're not walking it alone. He's here with you, and so am I." He nodded and squeezed her hand. "See you at lunch. I'll bring us something."

"You don't have to do that. Or be so nice." Kate knew her pain meds were messing with her head when butterflies fluttered in her stomach.

"I know, but I'm investing more than cash in this venture, Madame Partner." He winked. "Are you sure you're okay here alone?"

"I've already broken my arm. What more could go wrong?"

"I'll see you around noon with lunch, Katie. Stay safe." Will squeezed her hand again and headed for his truck. Once he climbed in, he rolled down the passenger window. "Barbecue okay? Vinegar or sauce?"

"Yes, and vinegar."

"Perfect." He started the truck and backed out. After he shifted gears, he waved.

Kate laughed. At least they had a taste for barbecue in common.

Once Will had gone, Kate decided to explore the library in the turret. She climbed the spiral staircase from the second floor into the center of the circular room. She smiled. It was like being welcomed by old friends into the heart of the house. She ran her finger over the dusty spines until she found her favorite,

Rebecca by Daphne Du Maurier. She brought it down and found a comfy seat on the red velvet settee to read.

Will pulled into his spot at the hardware store. The bell jangled as he entered.

"Good morning, Billy. Got our Katie settled then?" Dad was counting yesterday's receipts on his ancient paper strip calculator.

"She insisted on going to the house. Mom had her move out of the motel and into our guest room." Will adjusted some products on the shelves as he looked for the right primer for Katie's garage. "She helped Katie get dressed this morning."

Dad laughed. "That's my Maddy. She's taken in another stray. Or maybe she has an ulterior motive, Son. Don't tell me there's no attraction there."

Will remembered the feel of Katie's arm and her hand on his palm. Attraction? Not that he'd confess to his dad at this early stage anyway. "She's my business partner." He selected the primer he needed for Katie's garage.

"Many a romance blooms from a business partnership, Billy. Don't let her get away."

"Ah, Dad. She's hurt and overwhelmed by the needs of that house. I don't think she's thinking about romance." He set the primer on the counter. "Strange thing happened at the house last night. The graffiti on the garage doors bled completely through the paint Katie had applied."

Dad looked at the primer. "This stuff should cure that."

"Dad, it completely bled through it, like it had been repainted." Will wasn't a superstitious man, but Adams had a particular acclimation to all things Bell Witch. *Could it be a return of the infamous spirit Kate?*

"The vandals probably used an enamel that repelled the paint Katie used." Dad looked up at Will.

Will shrugged.

"Come on. You don't really believe all that nonsense, do you?"

"Just saying, Dad. It's pretty spooky."

Dad looked down at the paper tape and back to his numbers. "Darn it. See what you did dragging up the Bell Witch, no relation? Now I gotta start all over."

Will rolled his eyes and headed back to the stock room to put out some more summer project products on the shelves.

In his mind's eye he could still see Katie in her driveway, that graffiti over her shoulder and her arm in a cast. She'd had the same look on her face that he remembered from the last time she'd been in Adams to visit her aunt. They'd been friends, playmates as small children and confidantes as older children. He loved her then, his first crush. Then she'd gone away and hadn't come back until now. But she was the same Katie. He felt that heart tug from those years ago before high school and college. Had she felt the same?

"Billy, you gonna run down to Nashville for me?"

Will returned to the counter. "That's why I'm here and not on Spring Street."

His dad gave him the details of the order he needed picked up from his supplier in Nashville. Will grabbed up the invoice and headed out to the truck. Then he had an idea. He called the last number in his phone log.

"Hello? This is Kate."

"It's Will. Listen, I'm headed to Nashville for Dad. Want to come along? We could go by your storage facility and pick up your vacuum and anything else that would fit in my truck." Will hoped he wasn't being presumptuous.

"That sounds like a great idea. I can't really do much here with one arm and no vacuum. Honestly, I fell asleep reading a book. I'm not sure I feel like doing anything but going to sleep. I should have taken your mom up on staying at your house for the day." She paused. "When are you going?"

"Now. I'm in the truck headed to your house. I'll pick you up out front."

Two to four hours with Katie in his truck. Time to see if she remembered him as keenly as he remembered her.

He pulled up in front of the old house as Katie was stepping out onto the large wraparound porch. Locking the door, she headed for the truck where Will waited to open the door for her.

"My knight in shining Armor-all?"

Will chuckled. "It's what all the knights use these days to keep their trucks shiny."

Chapter 6

Returning to Nashville …

Kate struggled with the seatbelt. Will reached around her and pulled it out, so she could snap it into the buckle. She felt a blush creep up her neck at the surprising intimacy of such an ordinary moment. His nearness and his spicy aftershave tickled her heart. Oh yes, she remembered those summer days she spent in Adams with him. They'd climbed old trees, sat on the porch swing for hours, and walked the woods together. And yes, she'd cried at leaving him at the end of each summer vacation. This was different. Blushing at his nearness was a sign of a grown-up emotion at his closeness.

Then her mom got sick, and they didn't return to Adams to spend time with her great-aunt anymore. Will - she'd called him Billy then - slipped to the back of her mind. She never met another boy who could measure up to her summer boyfriend, even though she wasn't aware she was comparing them to him.

Now, here he was beside her. Despite the heartbreak of losing Brian as a result of being less than an hour's drive away, her heart felt mended in Will's presence. He could also have a girlfriend. He wore a college ring from Tennessee Tech and an engineer's ring on his pinkie like her dad had. No wedding ring at least. He lived with his parents, so likely no live-in girlfriend. Her only question was: *Did he feel the same way after all these years?*

Will turned the truck onto the I-24 ramp headed southeast to Nashville.

"So, you went to Tech? I didn't know they had degrees in Hardware Store Handyman."

"I'll have you know my degree is in civil engineering with an emphasis in structures." He stole a glance her way and grinned.

"Another term for handyman?" Kate knew she was baiting him, but that's what they always did when they were kids too.

"Only on your project. We may have to get down to the structure to build it back up." He put his elbow on the open window.

"Ow! That sounds expensive."

"That's what happens when you hire an engineer. Who's just a handyman now?" His deep laugh filled the truck cab.

"Okay, you win this round, Mr. Civil Engineer." Kate smiled and laid her head back on the headrest. *It was so good to be with him in this truck on this highway.*

Jerry Reed's voice exploded from the radio singing "East Bound and Down."

Will and Kate sang along at the top of their voices as they headed eastbound. They knew all of the words. At the end of the song, they both burst into laughter.

"Some things haven't changed, have they? You do

remember me, don't you?" Will glanced over to her.

"I didn't at first. I always called you Billy, and you weren't quite so tall last time we were together. Those times were the best ones of my life, Will."

"Mine too. How come you never came back?"

"Mom got cancer and fought it for a long time. She passed away when I was sixteen. Dad died in a car accident when I was eighteen. I went to Belmont for music business. Mom and Dad's estate paid for college, but working on Music Row was taking too long to get any traction in the field. Then Great-Aunt Katharine passed." Kate wiped away a tear. "I've been in and out of Adams for years while she wasted away at Whitehaven. Never stayed long enough or had the luxury of looking you up. I was always here in crisis mode if you know what I mean."

"Ah, Katie. Your life has not been easy. While we're confessing, I never stopped looking for you and your dark red ponytail." He reached over and gave it a pull. "Imagine my surprise when you rang my bell ..."

"No relation!" They both recited and laughed.

"... and I found you on the other side of the hardware counter."

Kate murmured, "And here we are. Making that long drive to Nashville."

"What about a long drive? It's less than an hour or so, depending on the traffic at the I-65 juncture."

Kate shook her head. "I know that, but my boyfriend dumped me because he said Adams was too far away to continue our relationship."

"You've got to be kidding. He dumped you over less than an hour drive?" He scrunched his eyebrows together in concern. "He wasn't worth the drive then."

"My heart has come to that conclusion lately. It hurt for a while though."

He gave her a smile. "I figure God knows better than me who I should marry. Until He brings her into my life, there's just no reason to date the wrong girl and get hurt."

"Wise philosophy. I've got too much to do to get wrapped up in another man." Kate watched his reaction. She was gratified to see him flinch a bit. "Unless, of course, God drops a man into my lap, so to speak."

Will grinned and gave a chuckle. "Well, you never know what God will do next, do you?"

They came to Briley Parkway, and Kate guided Will to the storage facility with her things on Dickerson Pike. When they arrived, Will opened the truck door for Kate and helped her out. When they came to her storage space, Kate handed her key to Will who unlocked the padlock and shoved the garage door up for her.

Kate maneuvered through the furniture and boxes until she found her vacuum cleaner.

"Here it is, Will."

"Look around and decide what else you could use in Adams."

While he carried the vacuum out to his truck, Kate looked into boxes, which wasn't easy with only one arm. *So much stuff leftover from my past life. Was any of it worth anything to anyone?* She plopped into her favorite chair and laid her head back. The pain meds had kicked in, finally. But now all she wanted was to sleep.

A gentle touch to her good arm woke her. She opened her eyes to Will's face inches away from hers.

"Are you okay?" He brushed hair back from her

face. "You scared me. I thought maybe you'd taken too much painkiller."

He was so close to her. She could easily have kissed him. Instead, she pushed him back. "I'm sleepy. All these memories overwhelmed me."

"Nice chair. Do you want to take it with us?"

"I'd like that, Will. It clearly wouldn't fit in my little car." She smiled at him.

He stood up then from his crouched position. "Why don't I go pick up Dad's order and you sort through things here? You can decide if any of it needs to go back with us. We can fit it in around Dad's stuff."

Kate nodded. "It hasn't been long since I dumped it here. I should be able to go through it while you're gone. Might even get in a nap."

Will stared into her eyes. Then he bent down and gave her a friendly kiss on the top of her head. "Be safe. I'll be back soon."

In a blink he was gone, leaving Kate stunned. *Does he have feelings for me like I have for him?* It was hard to know if she still had a little girl crush or was developing a big girl love for him. *Oh, but how safe he makes me feel.*

While he was gone, Kate poked around in her boxes and threw out more junk she didn't need. She was able to let go of more of her stuff now that she had a clearer idea of what her life in Adams might look like. In particular, no Brian Montgomery or any of the mementos she'd saved from her time with him. Movie ticket stubs, pressed flowers, notes, they all went in the trash bag she'd brought with her. She also threw out programs from shows she'd seen at TPAC in Nashville, Preds hockey programs, Sounds memorabilia, and napkins from other Nashville sites.

Moving furniture was beyond her physical capability with a broken arm. She'd have to depend on Will. Kate decided to take the chair, an end table, and a desk and wheeled chair, if Will had sufficient room in the truck bed. The big master bedroom would hold all of that.

Should I take my bed? It wouldn't be as musty and dust laden as Aunt Katharine's old bed. She'd already taken her own pillows and sheets.

The couch would have to wait for another day. Or until she was tired of paying for it to sit in storage. She lay down on it and promptly fell asleep.

She heard a voice near her ear, like the high-pitched whir of a mosquito.

"Kate Batts is your great-great-grandmother."

No!

"You can't deny family."

It's not true!

"You're named for her along with one from every generation of women."

That can't be right!

"You know it. And Will Bell is related to old Jack Bell despite their protests. How could you and Will have any chance at happiness?"

Kate jerked awake. She peered around the couch and searched throughout the storage bay for a source of the voice.

Chapter 7

Moving more of it …

Will didn't see her in the storage unit. "Katie?"

He poked around the boxes and furniture until he got to the back. There, on the couch, she was fast asleep. His personal Sleeping Beauty. She cradled her arm with the cast. *It must hurt. Her first day back in Adams, and I managed to hurt her already.*

It was just like the summers she visited her great-aunt. One summer she'd fallen in the creek and hit her head on a rock. She'd nearly drowned before he dragged her out of the water. Then there was the summer when the rope swing broke as he pushed her toward the sky. She had a broken clavicle that time. They rolled down a hill once, and she'd found a patch of poison ivy at the bottom. Every summer it was something near catastrophic. They'd planned to stay the night in the Bell Witch Cave the next summer she came, but she never returned after her mom's diagnosis.

Just as well. It might have been wrong to spend the night together anywhere by the time that summer had rolled around. She'd moved on, and he guessed he had too. Except, he hadn't, not really.

Will leaned over her and kissed her. She stirred and opened her eyes.

"So, it actually works then." Will took a seat on the floor. "I always wondered if kissing the sleeping beauty would awaken her."

"But then the sleeping beauty doesn't get to appreciate the kiss, does she?" Kate struggled to a sitting position on the couch. "You don't have to sit on the floor."

"You left yourself wide open to being burglarized or assaulted with the door open like that." What if she'd been hurt worse than he'd already hurt her?

"Will, I'm fine. What is that amazing smell? Whitt's Barbeque?"

"With vinegar sauce. I noticed a picnic table under a tree in the parking lot. I also brought sodas and chips."

When she smiled, her eyes lit up. "Let's eat then."

He helped her up from the couch. She squeezed his hand, and they swung their arms like they had when they were children. With a quick stop at the truck for the food, they hurried across the parking lot to the tree-shaded table.

Kate enjoyed the BBQ. That voice haunted her as she looked into his dark brown eyes. Could they ever be happy if the voice from her dream was right?

After eating, they lazed under the tree.

"I guess we need to get Dad's order back to him. Have you decided what you want to take back to Adams?"

"Depends on how much room you have left in the truck." Kate shaded her eyes, so she could look up into his. "I do remember you, by the way. I remember you were always getting me hurt."

"I remember that too." Will began picking up the trash. "And even though I haven't seen you in fifteen years, I still managed to break your arm."

"You know what they say." Kate quirked an eyebrow at him. "You only hurt the ones you love."

Will leveled his eyes at her and took her hand. "Then I must love you a vicious amount, Katie Winslow."

Kate's stomach flip-flopped, and she laughed. "That's okay by me as long as it's only accidents causing the hurt." And not Kate Batts's Bell Witch.

Will looked as though he'd kiss her, but instead stood up and took the trash to the facility dumpster.

Kate struggled to get up from the picnic table with only one arm to push up. Suddenly strong arms wrapped around her and pulled her up. She questioned him with her eyes, and he leaned down to her and kissed her.

"I've been wanting to do that ever since you rang the bell at the hardware store."

"What took so long, Will?"

"Guess I needed to be sure it would be accepted." He kissed her again. "Let's get as much of your stuff in the truck as we can. I hate for you to be paying to store your life in Nashville when I don't intend on you coming back here."

He placed his hand on the small of her back, and they hurried across the parking lot to her unit to pack the truck. A man near her unit helped Will load the couch, desk, and mattresses. He even gave them some rope to tie everything down securely.

When nothing was left in the unit, Kate went to the office to release the rental back to the attendant. The clerk refunded money for the unused time and accepted her keys.

"You say you're moving to Adams?" He put the keys in the appropriate cubbyhole. "Isn't that where the Bell Witch is?"

Kate laughed. "That's just an old story."

"Some of them old stories had basis in truth, lady." The man laughed. "I'll be here if you decide to move your stuff back."

Kate shivered. *Probably just the air conditioning in the office.*

She hurried back to Will's truck waiting just outside. Will jumped down and helped her into the truck. Once they were settled with seatbelts on, they headed back to Adams.

When they arrived in Adams, Will took her to his house. He led the way up the front walk and opened the door for her.

"Smells like Mom's already cooking dinner." He escorted her to the kitchen. "Mom, is that spaghetti or lasagna?"

"Think it's lasagna as long as I have all the ingredients." Mom smiled and wiped her hands on the long towel around her neck. She came to Katie and hugged her carefully. "How was your trip to

Nashville?"

"We got all the rest of my stuff in the back of the truck." She settled on a bar stool at the kitchen counter. "Will knew just how to pack it."

"I should think so after eight semesters at Tech. I swear the back of that truck is Mary Poppins's carpet bag. I was always waiting for him to pull a floor lamp out of nothing."

Katie laughed while Will's face grew hot. His mom gave him a knowing smile.

"I see how it is. Now I've got two women picking on me." He sat on the stool next to Katie. "Dad and Joe are going to meet me at the house to help me unload the truck."

"I'd forgotten Joe."

"My older brother. You want your bed in the master bedroom, right? Desk, too?"

"Yes, but I guess you'll need to tear down Aunt Katharine's bed to get it in there."

"No problem, Katie. We'll store the old bed in the attic." He smiled. "I'll vacuum the room thoroughly before we set up the new bed. Might even be room for the couch in there under the windows."

"Do you think so?" Katie's eyes searched his.

"We'll give it a try. We can always move it if you feel too crowded." Will stood and swiped a baby carrot from the bag on the counter. "I'll be back, Mom. Katie may need a nap before dinner."

His mom slapped his hand when he went back for another carrot. "You'll ruin your dinner, boy."

"You always said I could have a carrot if I wanted a snack before dinner."

"Pshaw, Billy."

Will wanted to kiss Katie goodbye, but he didn't know how comfortable she'd be with Mom as a witness. "Keys to the house? If you give me your car keys, we can unload your car too."

Katie rummaged in her bag and drew out a key ring filled with more keys than any one person should carry, except for a school janitor. "Here, I'll pull out the ones you need." She tried to take the key ring apart, but having only one useful hand made that difficult.

Mom pulled a key ring from the junk drawer. "Show me which ones he needs, and I'll put them on this ring." She made short work of the jumble. "Do you really need any of these other keys?"

Katie's face grew red. "They represent doors that opened to me at some point in my life. They're mementos of where I've been."

Mom reached across the counter and squeezed her hand. "You don't need them all in your purse, sweetheart. It'll injure your shoulder. I bet we could make you a memory board to hang them on."

Will started to laugh as took the selected keys. "It's gonna hurt her shoulder? Mom, we are so past gonna." He pointed at Katie's arm. "But it's a good idea. I better go, or you'll be eating the lasagna without me and Dad. Joe will probably want to get home to Sally too. Katie, I'll be back." He winked at her, rather than giving her the kiss he was hankering to give her.

When Will pulled up to Katie's house, Dad lounged in the swing, and Joe sat on the top step of the front porch. Will hopped out of his truck and jogged up the walk.

"Hey, guys, thanks for your help. Katie and I really

appreciate it." Will pulled the junk drawer key ring out of his jeans pocket and unlocked the front door for them.

"'Katie and I' is it?" Joe slapped him on the back. "She's been in town, what, three whole days?"

"We've known each other since we were kids." Will stepped inside and gasped. "Oh, no! Who did this?"

Dad and Joe filed in behind him at his exclamation.

The inside of the house had been ransacked and the walls sprayed with foul graffiti. Will dashed his hat into the floor then ran his hand through his hair. His heart sank. One more thing they'd have to conquer before Katie could open her B & B. When he closed the front door, he saw it again. The same graffiti as the garage door, a Bell Witch.

Dad scratched his head. "The front door was locked. We tried it in case you'd come in from the back alley."

Will raced to the back door. Locked as well. He went out into the garden through to the garage. That door was locked too. Mayhem reigned in the garage, including Victorian Seaside teal-gray paint splashed on Katie's compact car.

"Oh, no! How dare they ruin her car?" With a hand to his face, he prayed. *Lord, help us resolve this mess. And keep me calm. And help me tell Katie appropriately.*

He used Katie's key to open the door of the car. Marks around the keyhole showed someone had tried to pick the lock. The things inside looked undisturbed. Then Will went to the back of the car. Scratches and grooves showed someone had tried to pry the trunk open or jimmy the lock. Will opened the trunk. All was well. Frustration probably had resulted in the car's paint bath.

Will called the Robertson County Sheriff's Department and talked to dispatch.

He grabbed Katie's suitcase and several other things from the trunk and carried them to the house. Joe and Dad had the bed frame in hand.

"I can't believe it! What a mess!" Will's dad shook his head.

"It's worse. Her car's been scratched up, and her new can of paint is all over it."

Joe set his end down and wiped his face. "Katie is not going to be happy to see this mess. Are the sheriffs on their way?"

Will nodded. *And they'd better have some rational explanation for this, not some spooky Bell Witch stuff.*

"Good." Joe picked up the frame again. "Where does she want this?"

"Upstairs." Will took her things up the stairs to the master bedroom. On the floor outside the bedroom was a circle around a pentagram with candles burned at each point. A line of chalk covered the threshold. Will took a quick picture to send to the sheriff's department.

Dad scuffed the line of chalk. He muttered something unintelligible about curses and witches. "What is wrong with some people? No one should be doing this in our small town."

A knock on the front door announced the arrival of officers from the Robertson County Sheriff's department.

Dad and Joe brought in the rest of the furniture and boxes while Will talked with the officers and took pictures of the damage.

After taking Will's statement, Officer Trey Thompson flipped his notebook closed. "We'll have the forensic team here first thing tomorrow. Try not to disturb the scene more than you must."

Will nodded. "Thanks, Trey. I already touched all the doorknobs trying to see how the vandals entered. I guess any prints are unusable now."

"No worries, Will. You'd be surprised what those guys can do. Try to keep your activity confined to where the furniture is going."

"Gotcha."

Will vacuumed the bedroom with Katie's newer vacuum, as he'd promised. Then they wrangled the rest of the furniture up the stairs and into the room.

A text to both Will and his dad's phones announced, "Lasagna is ready."

Will's body slumped. How did the vandals get in? How could he tell Katie what had happened to her house?

55

Chapter 8

Vandalism reported …

Will drove Katie's paint-spattered compact car, and Joe had Will's truck. Dad took Joe home before returning for dinner.

After Will parked the car in front of the house, he walked up to the front porch. Katie was standing there with a hand over her mouth.

"What happened to my car?" Her voice was full of tears and terror. "It was in the closed and locked garage."

Will wanted to gather her to his chest. "That's not even the half of it. I'll show you pictures later. I've already talked to the sheriffs, and they're going to patrol frequently in case the vandals come back. Right now, we're going to eat dinner."

His mom came to the door and looked out on them. "My stars! Who did that to her pretty little car?"

"Dad's taking Joe home. He'll be back shortly. We just need to sit down and eat." Will removed his ball cap as he entered the house and hung it on the hall tree "Try not to worry. It will be okay. I'll change all the locks tomorrow."

Katie nodded and headed for the dinner table. "I guess a neighbor could have had a key." She sat and spread her napkin across her lap.

Will washed up at the sink.

"Is she gonna be okay?" Mom hugged Will's shoulders. "Katie's had enough trouble in three days than most folk have in a year."

"She needs a good night's sleep and a brighter tomorrow." Will carried the salad to the table and ran his hand across Katie's shoulders as he passed. He sat down beside her. "Looks good, Mom."

"And I helped." Katie giggled. "Guess there's nothing to do about the vandalism until tomorrow anyway. I'll probably retire after dinner."

"A sound idea, I'd say." Will's dad appeared in the dining room and took his place at the head of the table. "Let's pray. Heavenly Father, I thank you for Will and Katie's safety on the road. Thank you for this food and my wonderful wife. Bless it to our nourishment and healing. Amen."

Mom stood and cut the lasagna into squares. "It'll be easier if you pass your plates to me, and I'll serve."

Dad gave Mom his plate immediately. "Hey, I've been working all day while you been lollygagging around."

Maddy pursed her lips. "And what do you think I've been doing? Eating bon bons?"

Katie snorted her iced tea, gagging on a laugh. She grabbed a napkin too late to cover her *faux pas*. Her face was beet red. "I'm so sorry." She coughed a bit even still. "Maybe I should head to bed now."

"Nonsense. You have to eat. Give me that plate." Mom reached out, and Will handed the plate to her to fill.

After helping Maddy clean up, Kate and Will sat together on the porch swing looking at the pictures he'd taken of the vandalism in her house. It made Kate just about ill. The witch on the back of the front door disturbed her about as much as any of it. The words around it said, "Go back to your cave, Witch!"

"Are you okay, Katie?" Will put his arm around her shoulders. "How can I help?"

"I really think I need to sleep. Between the throbbing of my arm and shoulder and the vandalism, I don't think I can handle any more today."

"Go on up to the guest room. I'll send Mom up to help you." Will gave her a hug. "You're important to me, Katie."

Kate nodded and headed up the stairs to the flowery guest bedroom. That voice from the storage unit whispered in her memory.

A rap on the door startled her. She opened it to Will's mom. "Thank you for your help, Mrs. Bell."

"Don't call me Mrs. Bell. That's my mother-in-law. Call me Maddy or Mom. Okay?"

"I can do that, Maddy."

Maddy smiled. She hugged Kate and then began helping her undress.

"You know, Will is quite taken with you. But then, he always was. He couldn't wait for you to arrive for your annual visit with Kathy. The summer you never came just about killed him."

"I know. When Mom died, Dad just couldn't take two weeks to hang out with Great-Aunt Katharine. They didn't really get on, and he didn't want me by myself in Adams."

"You weren't never by yourself those summers. You and Will spent every waking moment together." Maddy pulled the nightgown over Kate's head and threaded the cast through the spaghetti straps. "Guess I can see that. It's hard when you're young and have no control over your situation. Just know that my youngest pined for you that summer."

"What about since? Did he have girlfriends? Go to prom? Have a steady in college?"

"Not really. Sure he went of a few dates, but you've been his one and only." Maddy stepped back and surveyed her. "Don't break his heart, Katie."

"I don't intend to, Maddy. Thank you for your help."

Maddy kissed her cheek. "Good night, Katie girl."

Kate woke with the sun on her face. Checking the clock, she jumped out of bed. *How did it get so late?* She pulled on a robe the best she was able and scurried down the hall to the bathroom. It smelled of hot shower and aftershave. *Has Will already gone out?*

She padded down the stairs to the kitchen. Maddy was praying with her open Bible in front of her on the table. Kate slowed her entrance into the kitchen.

"Sit down. God and I are nearly through." She never opened her eyes.

Kate poured coffee into the mug on the counter and added sugar and half-n-half and then quietly took a seat at the table. She stirred the mixture and took that first sip. Sighing she waited for Maddy and God to finish their conversation.

Mom had done this every day. She'd sing a little song when Kate was young: "Have a little chat with Jesus." Church every Sunday. Tithed every dollar. Her devotion didn't keep her from dying of cancer. Her dad died in that horrific car accident. Aunt Katharine had lingered in a haze of dementia. That wasn't better. Kate struggled with her faith and their loss. Now the house and her car had been vandalized. *God, why?* She never seemed to get past that question.

Kate felt arms surround her. She looked up into Maddy's eyes, so much like Will's.

"Why are you crying, Katie?"

"I didn't even know I was." Kate took a napkin and wiped away the tears. "You reminded me of my mom. She used to have her 'chat with Jesus' every morning too."

"Your mom was an inspiration to me. She lived her faith."

"Then why did God take her away from me? I could have used some inspiration too."

Maddy placed a cinnamon roll in front of her. "I don't know the answer. Only God does. What I know is that God directs our paths, so we'll become the people He needs in the paths of others." She took Kate's hand. "The Bible says we are fearfully and wonderfully made, Psalm 139:14." Maddy slid a paper from her Bible. "Thirty-five verses about being made by God for His purposes. Maybe you can meditate on these."

Kate took the computer page from her. "Where did Will go this morning?"

The screen door slammed on the front of the house

followed by a door thudding closed.

"Ask him yourself." Maddy grinned. "It will all be okay."

"Hey, sleepyhead. I've been up for hours." Will swung into a chair across from Kate. "Mom, any chance there's another roll left?"

Maddy grinned and brought him one on a plate. "Coffee?"

"Yes, please." Will sank his teeth into the cinnamon roll and then chewed in obvious pleasure.

She also placed a mug of black coffee in front of him.

"Thank you, Mom." He took a sip of coffee. "Katie, I took your car and had it cleaned. I met with the sheriff about the vandalism at your house. I started my work crew of buddies cleaning it up as best they can once the forensic team was finished." He took another bite and washed it down with coffee. "I suspect we'll need to strip the wallpaper down to the original walls."

Kate grimaced. "That all sounds expensive."

"It probably would need to be done sometime. Easier to do it without guests." Will winked at her. "I have no doubt that this will all work itself out, y'know Jeremiah 29:11."

Maddy smiled and quoted, "'For I know the plans I have for you,' declares the LORD, 'plans to prosper you and not to harm you, plans to give you hope and a future.'"

Kate frowned. "I used to believe that. Problem is He didn't promise sunshine and roses, did He?"

"Katie, it will all be okay. You'll see." Will finished the roll and coffee. "You need to get dressed. I'll drive you over to the house. I took some books of wallpaper samples over to your kitchen to help you decide. I've got locksets in the truck for your doors too."

"You're keeping a running total, aren't you?"

"No worries, madame partner. We'll be square." Will jumped up from the chair. "I'll go record my purchases in my computer accounts while Mom helps you get ready."

He placed a hand on her back as he passed, sending a delighted shiver up her neck. Katie grinned, but that voice from the storage place still echoed in her head.

"How could you and Will Bell have any chance at happiness?"

63

Chapter 9

Starting over …

Kate walked into the house and nearly fell to her knees. Foul words were spray-painted across the wallpaper. As if that wasn't bad enough, the words "Go back to your cave, Bell Witch!" were sprawled across one wall. On the back of the ancient wooden front door was a replica of the witch painted on the garage door.

"Oh, no! It's worse than I ever imagined, even with the pictures of the vandalism you showed me, Will." It was like Aunt Katharine had died all over again. She clung to Will and sobbed.

Will steadied Kate with an arm around her. "It's going to be okay, Katie. There's nothing here we can't fix."

Kate allowed him to guide her to the kitchen where she sat down at the table. "What about the library? Is it okay? Some of those books are old first editions."

"How do you get to the library?"

"On the second floor, there's a doorway that opens to a spiral staircase into the turret."

"I'll go check the library. Meanwhile, you take a look at replacement wallpaper."

Stacks of wallpaper books threatened to topple onto the floor. Will grabbed one from the top.

"This one is heritage paper, Victorian in particular. See if you can decide on a replacement. I suspect there's a century of wallpapers on the walls." Will scrunched down beside her chair. "Are you okay, Katie?"

"Can we afford your work team? I figured you and I would put in the labor."

"These guys I can pay with pizza or BBQ for lunch. They work cheap." Will grinned. "The vandals may have done us a favor by making us plunge right in instead of planning it to death. While Cole and the guys strip wallpaper, I'll replace the locks. Then I'll prime the garage door. I should be able to strip the witch from the back of the front door."

"How did they get in?" Kate shuddered. "I have to feel safe in the house."

Will stood, took off his ball cap, then ran his hand through his dark brown hair. "Don't know. I'll change the locks and check out the old ones. Maybe one was just loose, and they could jiggle it to gain entry."

"I guess I'll pick out wallpaper. I have no idea what I want." She opened the book. "I'm not good with too many options."

"Think about different choices for each bedroom too. As a bed and breakfast, you could offer different décor in each room. See what grabs your eye." Will winked and clasped her hand. "Take time to dream. It needs to be done sometime. Now's as good as ever."

Once he joined the crew in the living space, Kate grabbed her bag and pulled lime green sticky notes from it. As she paged through the wallpaper book, she stuck the notes on the margin of samples that grabbed her attention. She made notes on them as to which of the rooms the floral, damask, and striped papers should be used. Once she got into it, picking out wallpaper was fun. It also helped in tuning out the horrible ripping sounds from the living room.

Will found the door to the spiral staircase into the turret. He climbed the steps. It looked like Katie was the only person who had been up here in decades, maybe since Katie's mom's death. He fingered the books on the shelves. Sherlock Holmes. Edgar Allan Poe. Shakespeare. Dracula. Frankenstein. Robert Frost. Robert Burns. The collection was impressive with built in shelves to fit the curved walls. No vandal had entered this space. No damage. Praise God. He was glad he could tell Katie the library was untouched. Some good news.

Will wiped the primer from his hands and surveyed the cover on the garage door graffiti. The graffiti was covered now, but would it stay covered? It would freak Katie out if that graffiti showed up again. It was scary to think it might be something more than just paint.

After the vandalism inside and the pentagram outside her bedroom, Will was becoming concerned for Katie's safety. None of the locks were malfunctioning or loose. He had no viable theory for how someone could have entered the house without a key.

"Will, are we going to the wallpaper store?" Katie appeared behind him.

Will jumped and turned around. "Sure. Let me clean up."

Katie touched the wet paint. "Is this primer going to keep that creepy witch from turning up again?"

Will handed her a rag to wipe her hand. "That's the plan. We'll see once it dries. I also scrubbed the witch off the back of the door into the house."

"Did you figure out how someone got in?"

Will shook his head. "Here's a key to the new locks. They're all keyed the same. I put the rest of the keys in the back of your desk drawer in the bedroom. Hopefully a safe place someone wouldn't think to look."

"Thank you. You are doing so much to help me." Katie looked at the key in her hand and gave it back to him. "Here, you need one in order to work on the house. I might not always be with you when you need to get in. I'll grab one from the desk later. Wallpaper store?"

Will nodded and took her hand. "Why do you even trust me? I could have become a horrible person since we were ten. Fifteen years is a long time."

"We get along like no time has passed from those long-ago summers, don't we?" Katie smiled that smile that made his heart skip a beat. "I trust you because you've given me no reason to think differently."

Will wanted to grab her and kiss away any doubts she might have about him. It was way too soon to show the passion he felt for her. He didn't want to do anything to betray her trust. "We need to measure the walls before we head to the store."

Katie smacked her forehead. "Well, duh. Of course, we do." She squeezed his hand. "I think I saw a measuring tape in this old toolbox."

Will unclipped his tape measure from his belt. "Got one already. Those tools are pretty rusty. You could probably get tetanus from using them."

Katie laughed that sparkling laugh. "You could be right. Should I throw them away or put them on eBay for antique dealers to drool over?"

She was right. They fit together just as though no time had passed. Being with her made him happy. It was a satisfied feeling, as though he needed nothing else in this world. *God surely has brought her back into my life. Praise Him from whom all blessings flow!*

"Are we measuring walls?" Katie leaned back into the garage from the garden. "Where'd you go?"

"Spontaneous praise." Will smiled.

"Okaaaay." Katie quirked an eyebrow at him. "I thought I was the one on pain meds. You know, I have about an hour left before descending into pain or checking out."

"Then we'd best get a move on." Will followed her to the house with his trusty measuring tape. He began to believe he'd follow her anywhere, even into the Bell Witch cave, if she wanted.

When they returned to the house from their errands, a man was rocking in the swing on the front porch.

"Brian." Her breath caught. They'd been an item since college. He was going places as soon as he got that "big break." Despite dumping her over less than an hour's drive, he was still drop-dead handsome in that country singer way.

"Kate! I thought you'd never get back." Brian pushed his cowboy hat back and rose from the porch swing. "One of the crew let me in. Quite a mess you've got in there, Babe."

"Why are you here?" Kate felt Will back away from her. She turned to see what he was doing.

Will shook his head and hurried up the steps to greet him. "Will Bell. Katie's friend since childhood. Now I'm her contractor." He juggled the box of wallpaper and a bag of BBQ sandwiches from Adams Station Barbecue. Will put out a hand to greet Kate's ex-boyfriend.

Brian met him eye to eye then grasped Will's hand. "Brian Montgomery, good to know someone's taking care of my Kate."

She grimaced at his gall. Their handshake was too long, like a clandestine competition. Kate could almost smell the testosterone in the air.

"Will, our work crew is probably hungry. Why don't you go ahead in the house?" Kate climbed the steps slowly. "I'll see why Brian's here."

"Run along and do her bidding." He gave Will a mocking grin.

"You going to be okay out here?" Will's look of concern went straight to her heart.

"I'm fine."

Will gave Brian a squinty nod and disappeared into the house.

"What are you doing here? I thought it was too far to drive." Kate would have crossed her arms if one hadn't been in a cast.

"What happened, Babe?" Brian ignored her

question as he grabbed her good arm and steered her to the porch swing. "How'd you break your arm?"

Kate sat down in the swing. He sat beside her.

"I fell off an old rickety ladder." Her stomach clenched at his closeness. At one point, she would have gladly said yes to a proposal from him when they fell in love at Belmont.

"I had the day off, so I thought I'd drive up from Nashville to see my gal." Brian started the swing's motion.

"Ha! You dumped me. I'm hardly 'your gal' anymore." He had become too self-involved while starting his career and becoming bigger than life. "You don't need me."

His long legs created the arc of the swing. She couldn't compete with his control. She was stuck beside him.

"I'm man enough to admit I was wrong. The drive was picturesque and shorter than I'd imagined. That stop sign at the intersection of the cornfields caught me by surprise though!"

"I forget about it too." Kate didn't want to encourage him. "What are you doing here?"

He leaned in to kiss her, but Kate turned her head to avoid it.

"That's not a friendly greeting, Kate." His tone was dark. "After I drove all the way up here, at least I should get a kiss."

Kate jumped up from the swing, nearly falling. "No, you do not deserve a kiss, a hug, or to canoodle on the swing. You hurt me when you dumped me. We're through. Leave."

He furrowed his brow. "Give me a chance to set

this right. Or is your childhood friend also your lover."

She shook her head. "No, on both counts."

"You'll regret this, Kate." His tone was threatening. He stood and took each front step with deliberate motion.

Brian stalked to his fancy bright blue truck, meant for standing out on the streets of Nashville. Kate hadn't even noticed it when they pulled in. Will's truck was well-worn from hard work. Brian's truck was flashy, but Will's was honest and true.

She realized the same could be true for each man. What a revelation!

By the time they'd bought wallpaper for the living area and her bedroom and sandwiches at Adams Station for the crew, Kate was exhausted and in pain. Add Brian to the mix, and it was too much stress.

While Kate took her medication, Will handed out BBQ sandwiches and Coke to the crew.

He brought her the same. "Eat something. You shouldn't take that on an empty stomach."

She nodded and took a bite.

Kate woke suddenly when Will shook her shoulder.

"Are you okay? You dozed off on me."

His face was close enough to kiss, but she'd not give Will's work crew the opportunity to hassle Will or her.

"Maybe I'll go upstairs and nap on my own bed."

Will grabbed her half-eaten sandwich and drink. "I'll put these in the fridge for you for later. Do you want me to go with you upstairs?"

"Ooooh!" Catcalls by Will's friends embarrassed them both.

Kate's face burned. "No, I'm sure I can get up the stairs by myself. It's my arm that's broken, not my leg."

"I know that, but sometimes pain meds can make you dizzy. I wouldn't want you falling down the steps."

Laughter by the work crew drove Kate to get upstairs even faster. "Thanks for your help. I'll see you in an hour or so. Don't worry about the noise. I can sleep through anything when I'm tired."

Cole, one of Will's crew, called out to her. "Nighty-night, princess."

She heard Will hiss at him. "Stop it!"

Kate hurried up the stairs and closed the door tight. With her furniture in here and the dust in the air reduced, the bedroom felt like home. The bed was made with her own linens and bed quilt. No doubt Maddy had dropped by and added her feminine touch to the room.

On the desk, Katie found an old book: *An Authenticated History of the Famous Bell Witch,* by M. V. Ingram. She opened to the first pages and noted the original copyright was 1890. The pamphlet Kate had pulled out of her purse and left on the Bells' guest bedroom bed was also with it. *Yep, Maddy has been here.*

She began reading the pamphlet once she lay down.

"An evil spirit haunted the home of John Bell, Sr., beginning in 1817. Through many phenomena, the family was tormented by a spirit which said it was Kate Batts's Witch."

Kate scanned through the pamphlet, reading about the chaos performed by this 'spirit'.

"... But the prevailing account is that the Bell Witch claimed to be the spirit of Kate Batts, a neighbor of John Bell who believed she was cheated by him in a land purchase. On her deathbed, she swore that she would haunt John Bell and his descendants."

The pamphlet noted that the story was published in the Guidebook for Tennessee in 1933 by the Federal Government's Works Project Administration. The events surrounding the Bell Witch are taught as part of Tennessee history in seventh grade.

"There are many 'ghost' or 'haunting' tales in American History and when you investigate the many paranormal events, it is hard to overlook the Bell Witch. ... Former president Andrew Jackson was quoted as saying 'I had rather face the entire British Army than to spend another night with the Bell Witch' after he and some of his troops spent a night at the Bell's farm."

When Kate awoke, it was to an odd sound. A whooshing seemed to come from inside the walls. For a moment, she'd forgotten where she was. The pamphlet had slid across the bedspread to the edge of the bed. *Psyching myself out.* Then the sound occurred again, shaking the bedroom wall. Kate jumped from the bed and ran down the stairs.

"Will!" She stumbled on the stairs and grasped the banister with her good arm. "Will!"

Workmen's sounds ceased, and Will popped his head around the corner. "Katie? You all right?"

She ran straight into his arms and burrowed her face into his shoulder. "Oh, Will. The Bell Witch is here."

Snorts and chuckles rose from the work crew. "Oh, Will!" They mocked and then laughed outright.

Will pulled her into the kitchen and closed the door. "What's wrong? What happened?"

"Something is in the walls!" Kate pulled away from him. "I heard a whooshing sound from inside the walls."

75

Chapter 10

Someone else in the house …

Thunder reverberated throughout the house. Rain pounded on the roof. Kate jumped at the next thunderclap. Will hugged her close at the kitchen table.

"It's okay, Katie. It's just the storm."

She could feel his breath on her ear.

"I'll go check the attic. Maybe there's a loose shingle or board creating your whooshing sound in the walls." He let go of her. "Sit here and eat the rest of your lunch while I see what's up."

"No, I'm coming too. It's my house, after all."

"Well, come on." Will took her hand.

They climbed the stairs to the master suite level, ignoring the ribbing from the work crew. He went into Kate's bedroom and listened.

"I don't hear anything now."

"That doesn't mean it didn't happen."

He nodded, and they peeked into the other bedrooms. Except for the dust, there was nothing to see in any of them.

Will headed up the stairs to the attic. Kate hesitated. *What could be in the attic to cause such a sound? An animal? A loose shingle? An evil spirit?*

"Are you coming?" He held out a hand to her, just like he had on all their adventures back in the day.

"Of course, I am." Kate took his hand and climbed the steps behind him.

He opened the door to the attic and pulled Kate in with him. She flipped the switch to turn on the light. The bulb flickered then produced a dim glow.

It had been more than fifteen years since Kate had been in the attic. It was her quiet magical space, where she'd once hidden a diary. She'd played house in the attic when she wasn't with Will. Once her eyes adjusted to the dim light, she took in the familiar place now covered in dust, like everything else in the house. Her dolls lay on the trunk where she'd left them all those years ago, waiting for her return.

"Watch out!" Will grabbed her shoulders and pulled her back from an open hole in the floor.

"What is that?" Kate recovered from her startle. "A rag rug used to cover this part of the floor."

He turned on the flashlight on his phone and shined it into the hole in the floor. "Looks like more steps. But where could they go?"

"An old story said that the family treasures and children were hidden somewhere in the house during the Civil War to protect them from raiding troops. Perhaps there's a safe room down there." Kate edged closer to the hole. "Guess the only way to know is to explore it."

Will stepped into the hole onto the first step. "You coming?"

"Try to stop me." Kate felt the familiar adrenaline rush of an adventure with Will. She moved toward the doorway,

He took a third step and stumbled out of view.

"Are you okay?" Kate scooted back from the edge of the hole to give Will room to climb back up. "What happened?"

His head reappeared. "The third step gave way. Probably should wait to discover this safe room when it's safer. We could bring a ladder to put into the stairwell and aim a construction flood light down there. It's inky dark."

Will climbed out and helped Kate up from where she sat on the floor. "Let's keep this trapdoor closed for now while people are working here." He closed the door in the floor and latched it. "This might be the source of your noise in the walls. Wind could have come in under the eaves as the storm approached."

"You're probably right." Kate felt silly for her assumption that the sound was caused by something supernatural. "Guess I let my imagination run wild. When your mom was here, she left a copy of Ingram's *Bell Witch*."

"That explains a lot." Will escorted her from the attic and closed the door at the top of the stairs firmly. He threw the high latch bolt.

"That's how they kept me out of the attic when I was too short to reach. I did balance a chair on the top step once trying to reach it. That did not end well. The adults finally decided it was better to leave it unlocked than have me repeat that stunt again."

Will laughed out loud. "Girl, you were accident-prone even when I wasn't with you! That makes me feel better. Here I thought it was just me."

They arrived in the great room just as the last wallpaper was being stripped from the wall with a great hurrah.

"Anything else we can do for you while we're here?" Cole wiped the dust from his hands.

"Not now. I want to prep the walls before we put new paper up. You want to help with that later?"

Cole conferred with the other young men. "We're in. Just tell us when."

Kate stepped forward. "Thank you for your help. Sorry I'm a bit of a mess after all this."

"Hey, no problem, Princess. We thought you were his childhood imaginary friend, the way he talked about you." Cole laughed and the others joined in. "It's kind of a relief to see you're a real girl."

"And just as pretty as Will described," one of the other workmen added. "We thought you were literally his dream girl."

She felt the heat blaze into her face.

"That's quite enough from you guys. Thanks again. I'll call you when we need wallpaper to go up. We'll even pay you." Will walked with them to the front door. He waved as car and truck doors slammed and engines started.

Kate headed for the kitchen as he closed the front door. She grabbed her lunch from the fridge.

Will followed her through the swinging door into the kitchen and found her perched on a bar stool at the counter with the rest of her lunch.

"Are you okay?" Will pulled a bar stool up beside her at the counter. "They don't mean to act like jerks. They just can't help themselves."

"It's okay. I sorta deserved it." She finished her barbecue sandwich and took a deep drink of Coke. "I'm out of my depth, especially with one arm in a cast."

Will looped an arm around her shoulders. "We've made great progress today. Stripped all the wallpaper in the vandalized space, bought replacements for downstairs and your bedroom, and found a mystery in the attic."

"I'd like to see what's down in the hole under the attic." Kate turned to him and quirked her eyebrow. "What do you say?"

"I'll grab the ladder and the flood light. Let's go!"

Kate hurried up the stairs, flipping on all the lights on the way. What would they find in that dark hole in the middle of the house? How did it fit into the floorplan? When she flipped the light switch in the attic, the bulb sputtered and went out.

"Siri, add bring a light bulb for the attic to the list."

She stepped off the dimensions of the edge of the attic using her phone as a flashlight and grabbed an old pad of paper from beside her dolls. The pad of newsprint held her drawings and remembrances from her childhood. Kate flipped through it until she found a blank page and picked up a nearby pencil. She made a rough sketch of the attic with her measurements where she added the distance from each wall to place the trapdoor in the floor. She sketched in an approximate location of the stairs into the middle of the house.

Soon ladder appeared at the attic door, followed by Will. He laid the ladder down and plugged in the construction floodlight. Then Will unlatched and lifted the trapdoor and set the light so it would shine down the stairs into the dark hole.

Kate peered into the hidden staircase. "Good thing you didn't try to continue on those stairs. They're all warped and rotted."

Will placed the ladder into the now illuminated shaft. "You should stay here. Stairs are one thing. A ladder requires two good hands."

At her protest, he wrapped her in his arms. "My dearest friend and business partner. I would be remiss to allow you to go into this space on a ladder. I'll take pictures of whatever I find."

"That's not right, Will. It is my house." Kate filled with indignation and confusion as he hugged her. She knew he was right. But still … His hug only complicated her feelings.

"While I'm down there, I'll see what materials we need to repair the stairs so you can get down here as well." He released her and mounted the ladder. "It's damp in the shaft, Katie. That's what rotted the stairs. Probably not much ventilation in this space. I'd guess the safe room sits in the middle of the three bedrooms apart from the master suite on the second floor."

"I started a sketch of a floor plan from up here." Kate watched him with growing anxiety. If he got stuck inside the house, how would she help him?

"Great idea." Will reached the floor. He tested it before disembarking from the ladder. "Fourteen steps. How many from the second floor to the attic?"

"Pretty sure it's fourteen as well. I hit every one of them after my chair balancing catastrophe." Kate laughed at the memory.

"Which explains so much, Katie dear. There's a doorway into a long thin room. I'm going to check it out. If you can't hear me, I'll give you a call."

That same voice from the storage locker whispered in her ear. *You could close him in. Be rid of him! Avoid the danger of a relationship with the Bell family.*

The voice sounded real. She looked around the attic. Kate took deep breaths and tried to still her staccato heartbeat. She did a quick reconnaissance into the corners of the attic. *No one there. Were those her own thoughts? Or was it her imagination. I wouldn't want Will dead.*

"Are you okay down there?" Kate's voice trembled. "Will?"

She saw flashes from the room beyond the staircase. She took another deep breath. "What's down there?" Her voice grew stronger.

Will appeared at the bottom of the shaft. "There's a safe room here, for sure. It has some old wooden toys, a chest of silverware, and a few children's shoes. There's a door leading into the rest of the house, but it's latched on the other side. I can't open it unless I break it down."

"Then there is another entry to the safe room. Let's try to find that before we break down the door." Kate sat down at the edge of the hole in the floor. "Before you come up, pace off the size of the room."

"No problem. I got my handy dandy tape measure." Will disappeared into the room. "Probably about seven feet by nine feet. Wait, what's this?"

The resulting thud dropped Kate's heart into her stomach. "Will? Will?"

She received no reply. "Will!"

She dialed his phone. She heard his Jerry Reed "Eastbound and Down" ringtone, but Will didn't answer.

One arm in a cast or not, someone had to help him. She took a deep breath and climbed onto the ladder.

Chapter 11

Something in the walls …

Kate stuffed her cell phone into her jeans pocket. She sensed more than saw movement in the room below, but Will still did not answer her. Kate held her breath and stepped onto the closest rung. She wrapped her right arm around the ladder and leaned the left shoulder and cast against it. She slid one foot down, clutching onto the ladder. At each rung, she breathed out a prayer.

First rung. "God, if you're here with us, protect us…"

Second rung. "… from unknown forces or persons who would hurt us."

Third rung. "Help me feel Your Presence."

Fourth rung. "Keep Will safe."

Fifth rung. "Help me get down this ladder without further injury."

Sixth rung. "Help me know what to do for Will when I reach him."

Seventh rung. "Help me hang on to this ladder."

Eighth rung. "Help us climb back up to the attic."

Ninth rung. "Forgive me for doubting You."

Tenth rung. "Forgive me for blaming You for the deaths of my family."

Her right foot touched the wood floor. She brought the left one down as well. "Praise You, Father."

She flipped on the flashlight on her phone to illuminate the darkness in the room. Will lay crumbled up against a wall on the floor with blood oozing from his head. Kate hurried to him.

"Will. Wake up. You're bleeding. What happened?" She pulled his overshirt off him and wrapped it around his head. The shirt may have been the same one she'd used as a sling only a few days before. "Don't worry. I'll get us help." She cradled Will's head in her lap as she dialed 9-1-1.

"9-1-1. What is your emergency?"

"This is Kate Winslow at 415 Spring Street in Adams. Will Bell is unconscious after an injury."

"Is he breathing?"

Will's warm blood seeped into her jeans. "Yes, but he has a head wound that is bleeding."

"Can emergency personnel access the house?"

"Yes, the front door should be unlocked. We're in a hidden room. They'll need to come to the attic and climb down into a hidden safe room."

"Are you also hurt, Kate?"

"No, but there may be another person in the house who attacked Will."

After what felt like an eternity, Kate heard sirens begin. Tears fell onto Will's make-shift bandage. She looked up at the ceiling. "Thank you, God, for hearing my prayers."

Soon she heard heavy boots on the stairs.

"Kate Winslow! Will Bell!" Men's voices.

"We're down here. The ladder is secure." Kate wiped her face with the back of her hand.

Soon she heard voices calling to her and the creaking of the ladder. A fireman entered the narrow room in full gear.

"Ma'am, are you Kate Winslow who called 9-1-1?"

She nodded as hot tears streamed down her face.

"Terrance Larson with Adams Volunteer Fire. What happened?"

"He was measuring the room, trying to determine how big it is. Then he was on the floor, unconscious and bleeding. Someone else must have been in here with him."

Terrance nodded and made way for the EMT with his equipment to get to Will.

Kate gently placed Will's head on the floor and stood to provide more room.

A second EMT, a woman, took her hand. "When did you break your arm?"

Kate looked at the cast. "Three days ago."

"You climbed down that ladder?"

"Yes, someone had to help Will."

An officer entered the room. "Officer Andy Lawrence, ma'am, with Robertson County Sheriffs. You told dispatch that someone else was in the house. Who would that be?"

The Bell Witch. For a moment, she thought she'd said it aloud. "I don't know."

"Let's get you back up the ladder."

Terrance took her good arm and led her to the ladder. He followed her up to be sure she wouldn't fall. Then he guided her down the stairs to the kitchen.

"We'll let the medical pros help Will. Do you need something to drink?"

"There's a Coke in the fridge." Kate settled into a chair at the table. He handed her the cold can and popped it open for her. She took a long sip.

"When did you know there was a hidden room in your house?"

"Just a few hours ago. We were curious to discover what was down there. We should have waited until tomorrow."

He handed her a napkin. "If there really was someone in the house, better to know it than to spend the night here alone." He smiled. "I'm just a couple of houses down from you."

Terrance had the most remarkable blue eyes Kate had ever seen and a megawatt smile. She might have said more except the sound of boots on the stairs drew her to the living room. Will was on a stretcher between the EMTs, still unconscious.

"Did you want to ride with him to the medical center?" The lady EMT nodded to her. "It's okay if you want. I just spoke to the Bells. They will meet us at the Tristar Northcrest emergency room."

Kate hurried to her bedroom and grabbed her purse. Will was already in the ambulance when she ran back down the stairs. Terrance waited for her at the front door.

"They're waiting for you, Kate. I'm glad we met. Maybe we can meet again under different circumstances."

Kate took a breath. "That would be great." The sheriff department was still on the scene, so she didn't lock the door. She hurried to the ambulance, and EMTs helped her up into the back.

The ambulance screamed down Highway 41 to Springfield, TN. It was only twelve or so miles, but Kate felt every twist and turn in her stomach as she watched the EMTs run IV lines into Will's veins and follow the stats on the machines on board.

Will's eyes remained closed.

Maddy and Uncle Porter met the ambulance and steadied Kate as she stepped out of the back at TriStar Northcrest Hospital. She'd been here for her broken arm too.

"What happened, Katie?" Maddy hugged her.

Porter moved the women out of the way as the EMTs pulled the gurney with Will from the back of the ambulance.

"Honestly, I don't really know. He was fine, exploring a part of the house, and suddenly he was knocked out. I think someone else was in the house." When Kate said it again out loud, anxiety coursed through her veins. Would she ever feel safe in Aunt Katharine's house? The trembling of unexpended adrenaline began.

"Come. Let's find you a coffee and something to eat." Porter drew Kate away from the gurney as Maddy hurried with Will into the hospital.

Kate ran her free hand through her hair. "Maybe I can find a ride back to the house. I need to see what's happened. The sheriffs were there when we left." She pulled out her cell phone to call a taxi or Uber.

"Put your phone away, Katie girl. I'll take you back once they have Billy settled in a room. I'll even walk through the house with you." Porter placed a hand on her shoulder. "Nourishment first."

They found the coffee shop in the lobby still open.

After coffee and cake, Porter's phone rang in that old-fashioned telephone ring tone. "Got you. We'll be right up." Porter turned to Kate. "Billy's in a room and showing signs of consciousness. Let's go on up."

When they arrived on the third floor, Maddy stood outside the room. Porter hurried to her and wrapped her in an embrace.

"The doctors are in there with him. He's a little addled, but they think he'll be okay."

A doctor emerged into the hall and gathered the three of them together. "We've stitched his forehead. He has a concussion. He's a little out of it, but conscious. He needs rest and fluids. Let him rest here tonight, and we'll reevaluate in the morning."

"Katie, say your good-byes and I'll take you back to your house." Porter held Maddy as she sobbed on his shoulder.

Kate wandered into the hospital room. A white bandage was wrapped around Will's head at his forehead. His eyes were closed. She sat down in the chair beside the bed and took his hand. Kate startled when his eyes flew open.

"Katie. Is it really you?"

"Yes, Will. It's me. I'm so sorry you got hurt."

"No reason for you to be sorry. Not your fault." Will squeezed her hand. "Glad to see you, but you should go home. Get some rest."

Kate attempted a smile. "You too."

"No problem. Morphine pump, so groggy." Will grinned and closed his eyes.

Maddy went back into the room when Kate came

out.

Porter pulled his keys from his pocket. "Come on."

As they drove back to Adams, Kate filled him in on the finding of the secret room and their efforts to explore it.

When they pulled up in front of her house, the sheriffs were preparing to leave. Kate jumped out of the truck before Porter had a chance to open the cab door for her.

"Wait! What did you find?" Kate waved her good hand to draw their attention.

A young officer strode across the yard to Kate's assistance.

"We met earlier. Kate Winslow?" He checked his notes. "I'm Officer Andy Lawrence. How can I help?"

"What did you find? Is it safe to stay here tonight?"

Porter lingered behind her. "I can take you to our house before I head back to Springfield."

Officer Lawrence extended his hand. "Good to see you, Mr. Bell."

"Andy, just call me Porter." He turned to Kate. "Andy was a helper for me at the store during high school."

Kate brightened. "Andy? Will's best friend from school?"

He nodded. "When I'm in uniform, I'm supposed to address the public with respect." Andy chuckled. "You must be Will's Katie. How's Will? Has he regained consciousness?"

"Yes, and feeling no pain." Kate sagged, with adrenaline expended. "What did you find?"

Another officer joined the group.   "Not a

dadblamed thing. Sergeant Mahaffey, Miss Winslow. Whatever the intruder used to hit Will, he took it with him. If you find anything amiss, call me." Sgt. Mahaffey handed her his card.

Andy handed Kate a card. "You're welcome to call me as well. I'd suggest not staying here tonight."

"Thank you." Kate knew from the heat in her face that she was blushing as she watched the officers leave.

Porter stepped forward. "I'm heading back to Springfield. Can I drop you at home?"

"No, I think I'm going to stay here tonight. Terrance Larson lives just a couple houses away. I've got two numbers for Sheriff's Department officers. Besides, whoever was here has left by now, and the vandals were here yesterday. What else could happen?" Kate gave an exaggerated shrug.

She waved to the sheriff's officers and to Uncle Porter. When she went into Aunt Katharine's house, she locked all the doors and made sure the windows were secure. She left the lights on in the first-floor rooms then went up to her bedroom. She had a nightgown with her. She used the strategies Maddy had taught her to change into it with her injured arm.

She threw back the covers and screamed.

A crowbar lay there.

Nestled into her pillow.

Blood and hair encrusted it.

Chapter 12

Evidence of the culprit …

The crowbar was a testament to a living human being having hurt Will.

Once she calmed herself, Kate called Andy Lawrence of the Rutherford County Sheriff's Office. Then, wrapped in a blue-striped robe, she waited for him on the swing on the front porch in the dark.

The blue and white strobing lights on the sheriff's car announced Andy and his partner's arrival. They ran to her and thudded up onto the porch.

"What's happened now? Are you alright?" Andy hurried to her with his hand on his gun.

Kate stood up. "I found the weapon you were looking for." She wiped away an errant tear. "In my bed, under the covers. First bedroom at the top of the stairs." Kate's hands were shaking.

"Go ahead and sit down. We'll go check out the house again and recover the weapon from your bed. This whole thing feels personal. Who would want to hurt Will and terrorize you?"

Only one name came to mind, and it wasn't the Bell Witch. "My ex-boyfriend was here this afternoon.

Let's say he and Will did not get along. He was also mad at me for not falling back into his arms after he dumped me." Kate slumped back into the swing. "His name is Brian Montgomery. He lives in Nashville. I guess he could be staying in a nearby motel." She gave Andy a description. "I may still have a picture in my purse." She stood to get her bag.

Andy's partner, Larry Creary, came out of the house with the crowbar in a large plastic bag. A second bag held bed linens.

"I'm going with you into the house. He could still be here. In fact, I remember saying that you shouldn't stay here tonight." Andy brought his eyebrows together. "Are you always this stubborn?"

Kate nodded. "I've been known to have that trait. Thank you for coming back."

"You do have enough lights on I see." Andy chuckled.

"I didn't say I was brave." Kate entered the bedroom. Larry had taken the bloody pillowcase and the sheets from the bed. She dumped her purse on the desk and pawed through the contents with one hand. Finally, she pulled a ratty-edged photo from among the keys and makeup containers. "There you have him, Brian Montgomery."

A voice called out from downstairs. "Katie! Are you okay?"

"I'm in the master bedroom."

The thudding on the stairs answered her. "Katie!"

It was Will, head bandaged and face bruised. She opened her arms, and he grabbed her and held on tight.

"Why aren't you still in the hospital?" Kate kissed his forehead.

"Mom told them she could take care of me at home as well as they could at the hospital. 'Course I don't get morphine at home."

"Sounds like Miss Maddy all right." Andy laughed. "You've looked worse."

Will seemed to process that he and Kate weren't alone. "Andy? Why are you in Katie's bedroom?"

"I found the crowbar that decked you hidden in my bedsheets."

Will released her. "But that makes it all pretty personal, doesn't it? Not a stranger."

"Good guess, Sherlock." Andy slapped him on the back.

Andy's partner entered the room. "That's pretty grisly, Miss Winslow."

"Billy?" Porter's voice called from downstairs. "We promised to take you straight home." His footsteps on the stairs echoed through the house. "Katie-girl?"

"We're in here, Dad." Will held his head. "Speaking loudly hurts."

Porter entered the bedroom, which was beginning to feel crowded.

"Could you take me back to your house tonight after all?" Kate pulled her robe tighter. "I don't think I can stay the night under these circumstances. We need to make the property secure, Mr. Contractor."

Will nodded with care. "Totally agree, partner."

"Let me get dressed." Kate swept them all out of her bedroom.

She shuddered when she looked at the bed. Her stomach turned just thinking about the bloody crowbar nestled on her pillow in her bedsheets. Kate pulled on clean jeans since her earlier jeans also held Will's blood, threw on a t-shirt, gathered her things back in her purse, and hurried back down the stairs. She locked the front door hoping against hope it would be secure.

Andy and Larry had already left in their patrol car.

Porter and Maddy sat in the front of Porter's crew cab pickup. Will sat in back. She opened the back door and climbed into the seat next to Will.

"What made you come by here? It's not exactly on your way to your house." Kate managed the seatbelt.

"Billy insisted. Especially when he saw the bubblegum lights from the sheriff's car." Porter started the truck and threw it into gear. "We've had enough excitement to last the whole summer. Think we could avoid any more trips to the ER?"

"Good with me." Will squinted as he spoke and held his forehead with one hand.

Kate reached over and grasped his other hand in hers. "Thank you for looking out for me."

"I'd do anything to protect you." Will's brown eyes gazed into Kate's. "Haven't I told you that I love you?"

Kate gasped. *What do I say to that? It's too soon for forever.*

Will stuttered. "You know I've loved you since we were kids. Best friends forever, right?"

"Right!" Kate breathed a sigh of relief. That was something she could agree to.

Silence in the front seat meant his parents must have heard what he said. Porter pulled his truck into their driveway.

"Home again. Everyone needs to just go to bed." Maddy hurried out of the truck.

The dome light illuminated Will's battered face

and his shocked expression. Kate couldn't think of anything else to say, so she escaped from the truck to the guest bedroom. She dressed for bed again as quickly as she could.

A rap at the door startled her. "Yes?"

Will's voice came through the closed door. "Katie. I didn't mean to make you feel awkward. I've always loved you, my friend."

Kate leaned her head against the door. As much as she loved him, it wasn't the right time to declare happily ever afters. "I know, Will. I just can't leap beyond friendship yet."

"I understand. It's probably just the morphine. I didn't mean to ask for more. Good night."

When Kate entered the kitchen the next morning, Porter and Maddy sat at the table.

"Good morning. Did Will do okay last night?" Kate poured coffee into the mug set beside the pot for her.

"Maddy was up all night sitting beside him. Probably should have left him at Northcrest." Porter stared into the distance as he stirred his cup, the spoon tinkling as it touched the sides.

"You know I wouldn't have slept at that hospital anyways." Maddy shoved her chair back and stomped to the coffeemaker. She poured a fresh cup and doctored it with sugar and cream.

"Guess that's not much of an answer, Katie. Long story short is if he leaves the house today, it will be to return to the doctor or the hospital or both." Porter gulped the rest of his coffee. "Can I give you a ride to your house?"

"Please. Let me pack up my things." Kate stood, leaving her coffee barely touched.

"Now, there's no need in leaving." Maddy grabbed her arm. "What he said in the truck last night, that's no reason not to stay."

"I'm not ready for that commitment. We're friends and partners in the house. That's all I can handle right now." Kate placed her hand on Maddy's and pulled away. "You can always invite me for dinner though."

"Your invitation is always open." Maddy's eyes filled with tears. "What should I tell Billy?"

"Tell him I'm adding a security system to the house and plan to stay there for now." Kate left the kitchen and hurried up the stairs before they could see the tears in her own eyes.

When Porter pulled up in front of her house, Terrance Larson sat on the top step of the porch. He hurried to the truck as they parked.

Porter got out of the truck to shake his hand. "Whatcha doing here this morning?"

"Smoke detectors. A state grant gives them to fire departments to install for free. I figured Miss Kate needed a few." Terrance pointed to a brown paper bag on the porch. "I also wanted to check on Will and Kate after the crazy stuff that went on yesterday. I heard about the crowbar from Officers Creary and Lawrence. They stopped by this morning to check on things too." Terrance grabbed Kate's bag and headed for the porch.

Kate took Porter's hand. "Tell Will … tell him … to get better." Kate wasn't sure what to say after Will's declaration. "I'll come by and visit him later."

"I'd best get going. I've got to open the store and

get someone to watch it for me while we take Billy back to Springfield." Porter gave Kate a shoulder squeeze. "Let me know if we can help in any way."

"Thank you." Kate watched until he pulled away from the curb. Then she turned and headed to the porch where Terrance waited for her.

"Things okay? Porter and you seem a little tense." Terrance followed her up the steps.

"Will's injured worse than anyone believed. He didn't stay in the hospital and probably should have." Kate unlocked the door. "Please come in. I'm hoping to not find any more surprises today. I'd be lying if I said I wasn't glad to have someone enter with me." *No more surprise declarations needed. What else could go wrong?* If someone or something was trying to scare her off, she wasn't about to let them.

Chapter 13

Losing one's head …

Kate motioned for Terrance to follow her to the bedroom where he deposited the suitcase on her bed. Kate stashed her purse in a bottom drawer of the desk.

Terrance motioned to her bed. "Do you have more sheets?"

"Yes. The problem is putting them on one-handed. I'm sure I'll manage it. I have to become more self-sufficient." Kate rummaged through a box Will had placed in the closet. Her bloody jeans lay next to it. A wave of nausea came over her. She made herself not think about them. "Here's a set. Why don't I get you started with the smoke detectors, then I can work on fixing up the bed." Kate noted that blood had seeped through the pillowcase to the pillow cover. Another task to accomplish before bed. Perhaps she should just buy a new pillow. Maybe someone could drive her to Dollar General. "Where do the smoke detectors go?"

Kate followed Terrance as he looked around the second floor. "By code, they belong in every bedroom and hallways outside bedrooms. If it's okay, I'll just go ahead and scout out the best places, then you can approve them before I fasten them to the wall."

"Sounds good."

Once he headed out to accomplish his task, Kate opened her suitcase and gathered the dirty clothes, then she grabbed the bloody jeans and the offending pillow. She struggled down the stairway to the washer and dryer hidden in a closet off the kitchen.

All but the bloody things went into the washer. She used the laundry sink from the earlier days of the house to pretreat and rinse the blood from her jeans and her pillow cover. *Will's blood,* she remembered. Luckily the blood had not reached the foam pillow underneath the cover. She dabbed at it with laundry detergent anyway. She used the back of her hand to wipe the unbidden tears from her face. Then she dumped the jeans and pillow cover into the washer and started it up.

While Terrance placed the smoke detectors, Kate called a home security company and began washing the inside of the windows. As she rubbed the years of neglect from the old window glass, she wondered how Will was doing. She missed him. Her heart missed him.

"What do you mean Katie moved out?" Will put his hand to his head, hoping to stop the pounding. "Why would she leave?"

"You don't remember, do you? What you said to Katie on the way home last night?" His mom took his hand across the table.

"I remember stopping at the house, and the sheriffs were there. Katie found a crowbar in her bed?" Will shook his head. "Is she okay?"

"Pretty rattled." Mom squeezed his hand then took his cup to the counter to refill his coffee. "Dad gave her the name of a security company, and they were coming out today to install a system to secure the house."

"You still haven't told me why she moved out, Mom."

"I don't likely know all of Katie's mind. I'm betting your declaration in the truck had something to do with it." She set down his mug and sat down beside him. "Do you even remember what you said to her?"

"I wouldn't lie to her. How bad was what I said?" Will racked his brain but couldn't remember the ride home. "What did I say?"

His mom sighed. "It was something like, 'Haven't I told you that I love you?'"

"And I do. But ..." Will put his hand to his head. "Oh, it's too soon."

His mom embraced him. "She told us she's not ready for that kind of commitment."

The front door opened and slammed shut, causing Will to grimace.

"Okay, Katie's at her house. I got Andy to fill in at the store on his day off. Let's head back to Springfield." Porter entered the kitchen. "What's going on?"

"Katie moved out because I love her." Will held his head in his hands.

"I doubt it's that simple, but if it is, give her time. Meanwhile, let's go."

Kate finished cleaning the inside of the windows

while the security company set up surveillance equipment and alarm devices. She had him set up the outdoor video system to appear on her computer and her cellphone.

After explaining the arming and disarming of the system and the video features, the security guy showed her the app on her phone. "You can run the whole thing from your phone. In addition, you have a panic button to press if an intruder is in the house. It's even personal security wherever you go. Any questions?"

Terrance cleared his throat. "I asked him to install a sensor that would alert the volunteer fire station of any sign of smoke or fire. I hope that's okay."

"That's great." Kate stroked a large check from her inheritance fund. Mom and Dad and Aunt Katharine would want her to be safe.

Kate escorted the security guy out. When she came back in, Terrance was waiting for her.

"Lunch?" He seemed almost shy. "After that, I could clean the outside of your windows and put your screens in. Do you know where they were stored?"

"Yes, to lunch, as long as it's takeout." Kate pushed her escaping hair away from her face. "I don't know where the screens are. I can look while you're picking up food."

"No problem. What do you want? The gas station deli has a great turkey club sandwich."

"Sounds good. Let me get my purse to help pay for it." Kate headed for the stairs.

"I talked you into additional monitoring. I can pay for lunch." Terrance's blue eyes captured her. Then he smiled that electric smile.

"Ok, you win. Turkey club, baked Ruffles, and a

Coke."

Terrance swept a great bow with an imaginary hat, which had to have a plume like the Three Musketeers. "I shall return with lunch, milady."

Her stomach flipped at his gallantry. Kate laughed. He was so easy to be with. Everything with Will was so complicated. He and she were always the best of friends, but they were also children then without the complications of hormones. That connection was still there, but now they were adults.

She walked with Terrance to the front door. "See you soon."

"Lock this door. I'll call you when I'm on my way back." He took her hand. "You need to be safe in your own home."

He looked as though he wanted to kiss her but shook his head, and the moment passed. Kate watched as Terrance drove away.

Despite Terrance's company for the morning, Kate felt lonely for Will's presence in the house. Of course, she loved him. He was her first boyfriend. He'd grown into a handsome, kind man. *Will said he loved me.* However, when they became partners in the house renovation, simple attraction had gone out the proverbial window. If things went south in their relationship, Kate stood to lose Aunt Katharine's house in the end. Falling in love with him was too easy. That door needed to stay closed until she could pay him back for all the work he was doing on the house.

Kate closed the front door and locked it. After stuffing her cellphone in her pocket, she headed out to the garage to see if the screens had been stored there. She didn't remember seeing them in the attic.

Kate pulled out the new key to all the doors and opened the garden garage door. The security system chime sounded as the connection was broken. Her lonely car waited there in the dark. She flipped on the light and looked for any place that could be used to store screens. After poking around in the corners and looking up in the rafters, she came up emptyhanded.

As she left, Kate turned and looked at her car. "I miss driving you too. When I get the cast off, we'll go on adventures again." She imagined a headlight blink in response. She closed and locked the door.

Where could those screens be stored? Could whoever boarded up the windows have thrown them out because they were in bad condition? Where else could they be? Guess she'd check the attic again.

Chapter 14

Finding more than screens…

On her way to the attic, Kate's phone dinged.

The text from Terrance read, "On my way back with food!"

Instead of the attic, Kate headed toward the front door. It chimed when she opened it. That one note made her feel safer.

Terrance pulled up and hauled a grocery bag up to the house. "I picked up some snacks for your TV watching pleasure later tonight." He followed her to the kitchen and set the bag on the counter. "You do have a TV, don't you?"

"In the garage." Kate pulled a bag of Cheetos and another bag of white cheddar popcorn from the top of the bag. "Ooh! My favorites."

"I had you pegged as a cheesy girl." Terrance lifted his eyebrows, Groucho Marx style.

Kate laughed and then couldn't stop laughing.

"Hysterical laughing is a sign of exhaustion. I'll bring in your TV after lunch. I know a guy who can get you set up with Wi-Fi and streaming this afternoon."

Terrance led her to a chair where she sagged and

managed to stop laughing.

"I bought extra Coke for your fridge too. Are you going to be okay here alone tonight?"

Kate nodded. "Clearly, I need to sleep in my own bed. With the security system armed, I should feel safe enough. Thank you for your help today."

"You need a dog." Terrance placed the sandwiches and two drinks on the table and stashed the rest of the drinks in the fridge.

"What do you do when you're not volunteer firefighting and helping your neighbors?" Kate took a bite of her sandwich. "Oh, that is good!"

"I work part-time for Clarksville Fire and do a little farming." He took a sip of Coke. "I do odd jobs, delivering things and such. My house is paid for. It belonged to my grandma. I have few real needs. I like to help people."

Kate could see he was a real catch, except for the part where he didn't hold a full-time job. Of course, neither did Will. She wondered how he was doing. *"Haven't I told you I love you?"* His words echoed in her head.

"Hello, Kate? Where'd you go?" Terrance was waving his hand in front of her face. "You must really be tired. You just blanked out on me."

"Sorry." Kate wouldn't tell him she was thinking about another man.

Once they finished lunch, Kate gathered a light bulb and a flashlight and headed to the attic. Terrance was on the phone with Cole about installing her Wi-Fi and TV services.

She shuddered as she opened the attic door.

Afternoon sunlight filtered through the window and highlighted the ladder sticking out of the door in the floor. Kate replaced the spent lightbulb and turned the fixture on. It illuminated the dark corners.

She did not find screens. However, she did find trunks of treasures: diaries and letters tied with ribbons. Albums of black and white photos. Scrapbooks of mementoes. Kate sat in an old rocker and enjoyed her great aunt's treasures.

When she reached the bottom of a huge cedar chest, Kate found a large, dilapidated cardboard box tied with a blue silk sash. She pulled the box out and untied the bow. She pulled off the top of the box and gasped. A lace wedding dress, yellowed by time. She pulled it out and held it up to her. *It just might fit. The yellowing could be washed out.* She whirled around as though dancing a wedding waltz with the dress hugged tightly. The groom's face in her imaginary waltz was Will.

As she folded and repacked the dress with care, a knocking sound reverberated around the attic.

"Is someone there? Who are you? What do you want?" Kate's voice quivered.

The attic door slammed shut. Then the latch slid into place.

Kate ran to the door and pounded on it. "Open the door! Don't close me in up here!"

The knocking began again on the other side of the door. Kate backed away. Hysteria rose in her throat. *Keep your head. Some real live person is trying to scare you. It can't be the Bell Witch, can it? Trapped, I'm trapped with no way out.*

"Terrance! I'm locked in the attic! Help!" She

backed away from the door.

Then she remembered her phone. The only numbers she had were Will's, Porter's, Maddy's, Terrance's, and Andy's. She dialed Terrance. Just as it connected, Kate stepped backwards, into the hole in the floor.

Will climbed into the back of Dad's crew cab. "He said I was fine." He slammed the door closed.

"The doctor also said you have a serious concussion. You need to rest and heal." Mom closed the passenger door and clicked her seatbelt. "We're taking you straight to the house so you can rest."

"Katie needs me at her house. I can't believe you let her just move out, Dad." Will's head hurt thinking about what trouble Katie could get into without him. "Besides, I just have this feeling that she needs me, now!"

"Billy, there's just nothing you can do about a headstrong woman. She's gonna do what she's gonna do. Best you can do is be around to pick up the pieces."

"I just have this feeling that she's in danger. Can we at least go by her house and check on her?" Will crossed his arms. *Twenty-five years old and begging permission to visit my friend. Getting time to move out of my parents' house too.*

When they pulled onto Spring Street, an ambulance was sitting at the curb, and EMTs were pulling the gurney from the back and preparing to enter the house. Will released his seatbelt and launched from the back seat before Dad had fully stopped the truck.

He raced across the yard and entered the house before the EMTs. His friend Cole stood in the living area.

"Installing Wi-Fi and TV service." Cole pointed toward the stairs.

Will shook his head to clear the dizziness and took the stairs two at a time. Terrance stood outside the open attic door.

"What are you doing here?" Will gasped. His head pounded.

"Kate asked me to help her get a security system in place, and I installed free smoke detectors." Terrance paused. "Someone else was here though. The attic was locked on the outside latch. She couldn't get out. I heard her call to me. Then my phone rang. That's when I heard the thud."

Will rushed in. *No, no, no.* He climbed down the ladder to Katie who lay very still at the bottom of the stairs. He took her hand, still warm with a steady pulse.

EMTs appeared at the opening. The tall EMT cautioned him. "Don't move her. Let us check her out first."

Will backed into the safe room as the EMTs came down. Mom and Dad appeared at the opening with Terrance and Cole.

Dad put his hands on his hips. "Trouble just seems to follow Katie, don't it?"

Dad's voice washed over Will. It wasn't all just fate and superstition anymore. Ever since Will's assault, the accidents seemed more and more deliberate. Being locked in the attic was a deliberate human act. *She must have been terrified. No way could she have forgotten the door in the floor. Especially with the ladder sticking out of it. And a new light bulb. Who is trying to hurt her?*

Will stood by as the medical personnel put a collar on Katie and strapped her to a back board. They attached guidelines to the backboard to raise her out of the stairwell to the attic. Will helped guide the backboard climbing the ladder with it. The EMTs and Dad pulled on the lines. Terrance and Cole grabbed the backboard and helped guide it onto the stretcher.

"I am so sorry this happened on my watch, sweet Kate. I'll apologize again when you're conscious." Terrance kissed her cheek.

Heat rose inside Will as his emotions flipped his stomach and blazed on his face as Terrance kissed Katie's forehead. "I'll be riding in the ambulance."

"But. Billy, you're supposed to go straight home." Mom grabbed his hand. "Come home with us."

"I love you, Mom, and I care what you and Dad think." He paused and thought hard before continuing. "But I need to be sure she's okay. She's part of my future, don't you understand?"

"That's a pretty big assumption." Terrance crossed his arms. "Who says she picks you?"

"Boys! You both need to grow up." Mom headed down the stairs with the EMT squad.

They carried the stretcher out of the attic and down the staircases to the ambulance.

Will followed her as close as possible. He'd not lose her again. He climbed in after the stretcher.

"Hey, Will. Take care of her. We'll continue this discussion after Kate's better." Terrance closed the ambulance doors and pounded on the back.

Will braced himself beside Katie as the ambulance bumped out of her yard onto the street. The sirens filled his head as they picked up speed on Hwy 41 to Springfield.

Chapter 15

Hospital musings …

Will dozed off and on in the chair next to Katie's hospital bed. She'd been unconscious since the fall two days ago. Terrance and Andy had come and brought small presents from the hospital gift shop. Will and Mom had taken turns sitting beside her. That's when it struck him that she had no one. With her great aunt, her mom, and her dad all gone, the house was as close to family that she had.

He still hadn't helped her figure out what was going on there. And she was hurt again, worse than a broken arm.

He roused when a nurse bustled into the room to check her vitals.

"How's Miss Katie this morning?" The nurse clipped an oximeter on her finger, took her temperature with a scanner, then typed stats into a laptop. "Any change?"

Will shook his head. "Not that I can tell."

"Her vitals are stable. She's just not conscious. The doc should be by this morning. He mentioned yesterday that he'd order an additional CT brain scan and an MRI to check for brain function."

Dread filled the room. *What if she was brain dead? Or what if she was not the same after this? Why did she fall backwards into the shaft?*

"Can I get you something? Coffee? Soda? Snack?" The nurse's questions startled him back to reality.

Will stood and stretched. "A coffee would be good."

The nurse scurried from the room.

When he turned toward the door, Katie's ex-boyfriend Brian appeared with an enormous bouquet of roses.

Will scowled. "What are you doing here? How'd you know she was even here?"

Brian smirked as he walked into the room and placed the vase beside Katie's bed. "Visiting the sick. Bringing flowers to my gal. Perhaps running you off." He settled into a chair on the opposite side from Will's perch. "I went by the house to check on her, and the work crew told me what happened."

"Katie made it pretty plain that she doesn't want to see you." Will crossed his arms and sat back down. *Work crew?*

"She's in no condition to throw me out though, is she?" His lip curled, and he shoved his cowboy hat back on his head.

The nurse entered with a paper cup of coffee, creamer, and sugar. "Here's your coffee, Will. Oh, the flowers are lovely. Where did you find them?"

"At the end of Katie's ex-boyfriend's arm." He pointed across the bed.

Brian stood and removed his hat. "Brian Montgomery, ma'am."

The nurse sized him up. "They're lovely, but Katie really should have only one visitor at a time, sir."

"Will's been here long enough. Shouldn't I get the next turn?"

Will stood.

The nurse put her hands on her hips. "I'm sorry, Mr. Montgomery. I think you should leave. I can feel the tension in the air. If I can feel it, it's not good for Miss Winslow's recovery. Please leave."

Brian put his hat back on. "Okay, for now. But I'll be back." His boots clicked on the tile floor.

"Well. He's pretty, but he's not nice, is he?" She frowned. "I think I'll leave a note in the chart about keeping him out of the room."

Will nodded. "I can agree with that."

The nurse hurried away in her Dansko clogs.

Will wondered if Brian was somehow mixed up with all the strange things that were happening, including Katie's fall. He couldn't imagine how, but he was sure it wasn't beyond him to do some of that stuff.

The nurse returned. "A reward for your diligence with our patient." She handed him a package of shortbread. "Let me know if you need anything else."

"Thanks." After she left, he tore into the cookies and enjoyed them with his coffee. He guessed he was hungry. But would Katie be okay if he left her to get breakfast?

Two men in scrubs entered the room. "Kate Winslow?"

Will nodded. "She is."

"We're from radiology. We have orders to take her down for an MRI."

Will nodded. "So I heard."

One man checked her wristband and scanned it with a code reader, then the other unlocked the wheels on the bed. They maneuvered it out of the room.

"When should I expect her back?"

The larger man with a beard read the orders. "Probably at least two hours. Go get breakfast."

"Someplace else." The second man winked as they rolled the bed toward the elevator.

Will laughed. "Right, hospital food. I got it."

He rode the elevator to the first floor. The sun blinded him as he entered the summer day outside the hospital. He'd been cooped up in that refrigerator of a hospital too long. Will shuddered as his cold skin met the summer sun.

As his eyes adjusted to the bright light, Will noticed Brian's flashy truck sitting beside his own not-so-flashy truck. The man exited the cab and slipped on the cowboy hat. *How I want to knock that thing off his head!*

"Will Bell. I bet they call you Billy in this backwater, don't they?"

Will shook his head. "Why are you here? Katie told you to leave her alone. She was quite clear."

"You know how women are. The more they say no, the more you got to have them." Brian laughed a dark laugh. "So, she and I still have something to finish before she starts anything with you."

Will clenched his fists at his sides. *How dare he insinuate...* "You are disgusting. Leave Katie alone."

"Or you'll do what?" Brian leaned back on the tailgate of his truck. "What makes you think she'll choose you?"

"We're the best kind of friends. Whether she

chooses me as more has yet to be determined. But she'll always be my friend. That relationship is certain. Can you say the same?"

"Friendship. That's fine by me. Just stay out of my way when I seduce her …"

Before Brian could finish, Will punched him square in the mouth. Soon they were scrapping on the parking lot asphalt. Fists flying, feet kicking, gravel flinging.

"Billy Chadwick Bell! You stop this right this minute!"

Brian laughed. "Must be your mama, Billy."

"And hospital security, boy." A security guard stood behind Mom.

Brian and Will stood up. Brian picked up his hat, dusted it off, and put it on his head.

Will straightened his shirt and wiped blood from his mouth with the cloth handkerchief from his back pocket.

The security guard slid in front of Mom. "What is going on here?"

"Is this about Katie? Are you Brian, the boy that dumped our Katie?" Mom crossed her arms.

"Sorry, ma'am, but she is my Kate. And I intend to win her back. Billy, tell your mama about the flowers I brought today." Brian poked his finger into Will's chest.

The security guard moved in between the two men.

Will shook his head and rolled his eyes.

"Who's sitting with Katie now while you two are rolling around in the parking lot? Don't tell me you left her alone. What if she wakes up alone?" Mom waved her hands in the air when she got excited. She was excited now. "Well, son?"

"They took her to radiology for an MRI. They want to determine the amount of damage to her brain from the fall." Will stuck his scraped hands into his jean pockets. "They're afraid she'll never wake up."

"Ma'am, can you vouch for your son?" The security guard had a grasp on Brian's arm. At her nod, he turned to Brian. "You're coming with me." The two walked across the parking lot.

"He's got no business here and no right to say the things he was saying, Mom." Will's adrenaline was still pumping from the fight.

"I hear you. You can only control yourself, Son. From the looks of you, I'd say you failed to do that. And you with a concussion at that!" Mom looked into his eyes, then took him into her arms. "I know how much you care about her. That's no excuse for a parking lot scramble."

Will nodded into her shoulder. "I know, Mom."

"Go home, clean up, and get you something to eat. I'll stay and wait for the doctor to tell us what the tests show."

Will puzzled. "Do you know anything about a work crew at Katie's house?"

"All I know is that Joe went out early after coming for breakfast. But that don't mean nothing." His mom hugged him again. "Get on home so you can come back. Take a nap if you need to. I got my Bible and novels to read."

"Do some praying too. They're looking for brain damage." Will hugged Mom tight. He'd be praying too. *And who was at the house?*

Chapter 16

Return to consciousness ...

Kate stirred and felt softness all around her. The last thing she remembered was being in the attic. She opened her eyes and saw white all around her. *I'm dead!* A beeping sound permeated her growing consciousness.

"Katie! You've come back to us!" Maddy grabbed her hand. "Sweet girl, we've been so worried."

Will's mom? "Maddy?" Her voice came out as a croaky rasp. She coughed, and Maddy hurried to bring her a cup of water from her hospital tray.

"Don't strain yourself. Let me go get the nurse." As soon as Maddy entered the hallway, she started shouting. "She's awake! She's awake!"

Katie stretched and everything hurt. The last thing she remembered was that voice and falling into darkness. *Where could that voice have come from? The Bell Witch? Why would that spirit haunt her? Where is Will?*

A nurse hurried into the room. "Miss Kate Winslow! About time you graced us with your presence." She checked her vital signs and her eyes with a small flashlight. "You're looking good for someone who's been unconscious for two days. You took quite a fall."

Kate tried to sit up.

"No, don't move until the doctor assesses your injuries. There's only so much they can know without your responses."

"Is that why I'm tied down?" Kate pulled against the restraints. "It's not because you think I'm crazy, is it?"

"Of course not. No one wanted you trying to get out of bed before we knew you were conscious."

Kate relaxed back in the bed. Maddy rushed into the room with her cell phone to her ear.

"Will's on his way. You've given us quite a fright." Maddy stashed her phone in her tote bag. She resumed her position in the chair beside Kate's bed and grabbed her hand. "I'm so glad you're okay. Will has been beside himself. He even got into a dustup in the parking lot with that cowboy."

"Cowboy? You mean Brian? He got in a fight with Brian?" Kate blinked. *I must have woken up in a different world if Will and Brian are fighting in the parking lot.* "Who are the roses from?"

"Must be Brian because my son isn't all that romantic. He'd never think someone needed roses if he was going to be there in person." Maddy stood and poked around in the bouquet. "Here's a card. 'To my gal Kate, Get well soon so you can return to Nashville with me. Love, Brian.'"

"Throw that card away. Sounds just like Brian. All show but not much heart. I would have married him if he'd asked before now. Take those flowers down to the nurses' station." Pain was creeping up on Kate. "Can you call the nurse?" Tears prickled the inside of her eyelids. She huffed and puffed to try to lessen the pain coming from her arm, her head, her back, from just about everywhere.

Maddy jumped from her chair and rushed out of the room. Kate closed her eyes and tried to think about anything else to deaden the screaming of her injured nerve endings.

Maddy and the nurse rushed in.

"Kate, what's going on?" The nurse checked the machines. "Are you in pain?"

Kate nodded, but it hurt more to nod. "Yes. All over."

"I'll hurry the doctor here. I told him you were awake. He should be on his way." The nurse pulled her phone from her pocket and made a call. "We need Dr. Gray here STAT."

Will pulled up in front of Kate's house. *What is happening here?* Several other trucks were parked out front, including his brother Joe's pickup truck. His phone buzzed as he stepped out of the cab. *Mom.*

"Mom, what's going on with Katie?"

"She's awake and in horrific pain. She's asking for you."

"Tell her I'll be there as soon as possible. I'm going to check in on Joe and his friends."

He hurried up the walk so he could get to the hospital sooner.

He found a work crew of ten putting up wallpaper

and painting the trim. His brother Joe was on a ladder in the dining area.

"What are you doing here?"

Joe put down his brush. "Painting. What's it look like?"

Will rolled his eyes. "No duh. Why are you here? How did you get in?"

"Ah, now those are worthy questions." Joe climbed down the ladder. "I knew you guys needed help. Who knows how long Katie will be in the hospital or how badly hurt she is? She could remain unconscious for days or months."

"Mom just called. She's awake."

"Great! Anyhow, I figured the best thing I could do to help you and Katie was to bring guys over and work on what you'd started. Mom had a key that Katie had given her, so she gave it to me. It's supposed to be a surprise." Joe wiped his hands on a rag. "Surprise!"

"Did they prep the walls before hanging the paper? Are they using the right glue?"

"Billy! Yes. These guys are pros. They agreed to donate their labor to help y'all out. Don't look a gift horse in the mouth." Joe grinned and patted him on the back. "It's all going to be okay. By the way, we found another surprise as we were prepping the walls."

Will followed Joe into the telephone alcove from days gone by.

"Look at this." Joe pressed in a disk hidden in the alcove, and a door swung open. "You'd been looking for a way into the walls. Here you go!"

"Did you go in?" Will pushed the door in a bit farther and found a dark narrow corridor with cobwebs strung on the walls.

"No. After all the issues in the attic space, I wasn't interested in getting stuck in the middle of the house. The rescue squads have been here enough already. Sally would have a cow if I got hurt, with the baby due soon. I still have fields to manage, you know. I can't afford to get hurt before harvesting."

"Got it. I'd go in now, but I need to get to the hospital. Don't paper over this just yet. Katie will want to explore this with me." Will stuck out his hand to Joe. "Thanks. I appreciate your help more than you know. I'll go check on Katie."

"We'll try to get this floor's decorating done by the time she comes home. Go take care of your Katie." Joe nodded and grinned. "After all, she's pretty much family, isn't she?"

Will nodded. "I'm sure hoping so. If she'll have me."

"Well, then, maybe it's not so certain after all." Joe laughed as Will took a swipe at him and missed. "Go take care of her, little brother. Give her my best."

Will jogged out to his truck and headed to Springfield.

When Will stepped out of the hospital elevator on Katie's floor, Mom was standing outside Katie's door.

"What's happening?"

Mom wiped her face with a tissue. "Katie's awake but in so much pain. The docs are in there trying to determine the extent of her injuries."

Will took her into his arms. "It'll be okay. She's awake, and that's something big. If they need to, they'll send her to Vanderbilt Hospital in Nashville. Go home and rest. I'll be here with her."

"You sure, Billy? I want to know everything. You call me."

"I will, Mom." He hugged her again and sent her home.

Doctors left the room in a hurry until Dr. Gray was the only one left.

"Here's what we know. The fall caused some brain swelling, but the tests show it's receding. She has a concussion. Now the problem is pain. We've given her sedation to allow her to relax while the body recovers. It may not seem like it, but Miss Winslow is a lucky lady. She could have had a break causing paralysis. Instead, she has minor fractures along her spine." He held the x-ray to the light for Will. "You can see them from the thoracic to the lower spine. I'm going to consult a friend of mine in Nashville about her injuries. She probably needs to go to Vanderbilt University Medical Center for better care."

Nashville. Brian's territory. Will shuddered. "I can go with her."

The doctor narrowed his eyes at Will. "You, sir, are still recovering from a traumatic head injury yourself. I appreciate your loyalty to your friend, but you need to take time to heal as well."

"If I'm just sitting beside her, wouldn't that constitute taking time to heal?" Will couldn't let Katie go to Nashville without him.

The doctor stroked his chin. "I guess you're right, as long as you take it easy."

"You got it."

"I'll make the arrangements to transfer her to Vanderbilt." His phone buzzed, and he swept down the hallway.

Will turned back to Katie. She seemed calmer with the morphine pump available for her pain.

"Katie, do you have anyone who has medical power of attorney?" Will held her hand as he spoke.

"No. It's just me. I'm alone." Katie's pitiful response nearly broke his heart.

"What about Mom? She could be your medical power of attorney. I'm concerned the docs at Vandy may want to put you in an induced coma. Then you couldn't answer for yourself."

"Could you call her and ask, Will?" Katie squeezed his hand and grimaced. "You'll go with me then?"

"Wild horses couldn't keep me away." Will sure didn't want Brian there. Brian radiated a desire to own and control Katie, not to love or cherish her. "I'll call Mom now."

When Will stepped out in the hall to call her, paramedics came off the elevator with a gurney and headed into Katie's room.

"Mom, Katie and I are headed to Nashville to Vanderbilt. Can you come? Katie would like you to be her medical power of attorney."

Katie cried out in pain as the paramedics moved her onto a back board then transferred her to the gurney. "Will!"

"Gotta go, Mom." He hurried to Katie's side and held her hand as they moved her to the waiting ambulance.

"I'll follow in my truck. Try to relax. I'll be there right behind you. And Mom is coming too."

"I love you too." She whispered to him.

Will nodded. "I'll see you there."

The paramedics slammed the ambulance doors closed. The siren began as soon as they started onto US-431S leading to I-24E, scattering the traffic to the shoulders.

Chapter 17

In Nashville for recovery …

Will ran to his truck, started it up, and headed down the same road. Unfortunately, the traffic didn't clear for his beat-up work truck like it did for an ambulance. When he reached the interstate, the ambulance was nowhere to be found. He set his speed at 70 mph, the legal limit in Tennessee, and traveled as well as he could to downtown Nashville, slowing in spots then speeding up in others.

Kate dozed on and off after the ambulance reached the relatively smooth road of the highway. She heard the siren, but it didn't interrupt her sleepiness. She dreamed of falling into the safe room. *Wait, that was real. Will wasn't there. But he was at the hospital. Where is he now? Oh yeah, driving his truck to Nashville. Why is he driving to Nashville? Oh, yeah, because that's where I'm going too. Vanderbilt. Where Dad died after his accident. Where Mom died. A place*

to go to die.

"Don't quit on me, Miss Kate. You still have living to do." A deep voice, an EMT?

"Will?"

"He's following us to Vanderbilt. You need to stay with me." A higher voice, another EMT?

"He's okay, isn't he?"

"Of course." The deep voice again. "Take a few deep breaths, Miss Kate."

"That's good. Her oxygen level is better already," the higher voice proclaimed.

Will followed the presumed path of the ambulance down US-431S to the main highway. *The ambulance probably knows the best path through the traffic.* He joined I-24E at Joelton and drove straight into the city. Traffic began to slow at the I-65 split. His phone's GPS app had him get off before the Titans's football stadium and take the Korean Veterans bridge into the heart of Nashville, past the honky-tonks and tourist attractions. He pulled onto the campus of Vanderbilt and into the parking garage across from the hospital. After he parked, Will raced across the pedestrian span over the street into the hospital.

At the first information desk he came to, Will stopped.

The lady in a smock looked up at him. "Can I help you?"

"I need to know to what room Kate Winslow has

been admitted. She was being transferred from Springfield." He drew in a deep breath to slow his heart from feeling like it was beating out of his chest.

The volunteer searched her screen. "I don't see her yet. They'll bring her in through the Emergency Department before they assign a room." She gave him directions to the ED.

Will hurried to the elevator, punching the down button several times. Giving up, he took the stairs instead. *I can't miss her. She needs me.*

He found the Emergency Department just as the door opened for a hospital bed holding his Katie.

"Will." She gazed up into his eyes. She seemed far away from him, adrift in a different reality. "Don't leave me."

He grabbed onto the bar beside her and walked with it to the elevator. "I'm here, Katie. Stay with me." He turned to the medics with her. "What's wrong with her? She was coherent when she left in the ambulance forty-five minutes ago."

"Are you family?" They settled the bed in the elevator and pushed the tenth-floor button.

"As close as she's got." Will grasped Katie's hand. "She's my girlfriend." Close enough. She was a girl and his friend. After this was over, he'd determine their relationship status.

"Paramedics said she coded in the ambulance. She's a little foggy, but as you know, she's also suffered a severe concussion."

Will gasped and leaned back against the rails on the back wall of the elevator. *She nearly died.* He'd never anticipated that consequence.

"Hey, are you okay? Were you both in an

accident?" The man motioned to his bandage on his head.

"Not at the same time, no." *Were they accidents or assaults perpetrated by the same person?*

At that moment, the elevator doors opened on the tenth floor revealing Brian Montgomery.

How did Brian know she'd be here?

"What luck to run into the two of you here!" He cocked his hat on the back of his head and gave Will a devilish smile. "I wasn't sure I'd get here in time."

He moved as the attendant maneuvered the bed out of the elevator.

Will followed the bed. "What are you doing here?" Will hissed under his breath.

"Same as you, I expect. After all, I'm her emergency contact." Brian raised his eyebrows. "Didn't expect that, didja?"

When the bed reached the Trauma Center, a nurse greeted the men. "Go wait in the waiting room. I'll come get you after she's settled." She pointed down the hall to a room with chairs and a TV.

"Great," Will grumbled under his breath.

They walked on opposite sides of the hall to the waiting room then chose seats on opposite sides of the room. Will flipped through a magazine. Brian flipped through TV channels, settling on HGTV. Finally, the nurse appeared.

"Only one of you two can go in at a time."

As she turned to go, the nurse nearly ran into Mom.

"I'm here to be Katie's medical power of attorney." Mom caught her breath. "Should I go in first to satisfy the need for a legal care representative?" She nodded at Brian.

The nurse stepped around her in front of the two men. "Yes, you should go in first. Men, you'll need to still wait here."

"What?" Brian dashed his hat to the floor. "I'm the emergency contact! I'm the one who should be going in first! How does your mom get to do this?"

Will tried to suppress a grin. "Katie asked Mom to be her medical power of attorney, that's why."

A hospital security guard entered the waiting room. "Is there a problem, guys? We want this floor in particular to be quiet. People here are really sick."

Brian reached down and plucked his hat up. "No, sir. No problem at all."

"Let's keep it down then." The guard headed back down to the nurses' station.

Will went to the coffee setup and fixed himself a cup while Brian settled in the corner by the window. He had his phone out and was talking into it. What was he doing? Creating lyrics? Recording a diary entry? Will shook his head and found a seat close to the hall.

Kate lay as still as she could as the nurses surrounded her, placing new IV lines and wires and cuffs to monitor her condition. She'd heard the medics say she had coded in the ambulance. Could it get any worse? She knew Will and Brian were in the waiting room, together. That alone created anxiety. According to Maddy, they'd already had a fight at the Springfield hospital. She hadn't realized until her time with Will just how much stress Brian created in her. She knew now that stress was not the same as love. Between the pain and the anxiety she felt, Kate would be happy to be asleep for a while.

"You may come in now, ma'am." The nurse escorted Maddy into the room as she left.

"Katie! You've given us quite a fright." Maddy pulled a chair over and sat down beside the bed. "How are you feeling?"

"Truthfully? Scared." Kate grabbed her hand. "I think I'm losing my mind. I heard a voice and knocks and all that Bell Witch stuff. That's why I managed to back into the hole in the attic floor."

"Now, now. I'm sure there's a logical explanation." Maddy patted her hand. "Everything will be okay."

"Brian's here too." Tears formed in her eyes. "Why is he here?"

"He's listed as your emergency contact."

"That must change. I don't want him even near me." Tears flowed down Kate's face.

"That's one reason I'm here now. The nurse gave me some paperwork to fill out to be your medical power of attorney. She'll witness our signatures too. That is if that's what you still want."

Kate nodded, which sent off waves of pain through her. She closed her eyes and laid her head back into the pillow. "Yes, Maddy. I trust you."

Maddy began filling out the form, asking Kate questions. Finally, Kate called the nurse to witness their signatures.

Once the signatures were legal, Kate relaxed. "Maddy, can you ask Brian to leave me alone?"

"It would be my pleasure, Miss Katie." Maddy tucked the power of attorney in her tote bag and strode out of the room.

Will stood when Mom entered the waiting room. "How's she doing?"

Brian headed for the hallway. Mom grabbed his arm on the way past her.

"Katie is in a lot of pain and quite anxious about what's going on out here in the waiting room. She asked me to tell Brian to go home and leave her alone." Mom gave Brian a stern look. "If you won't do that because she asked you to, I'll get security involved."

"What gives you the right to tell me to leave?" Brian hooked his thumbs in his jeans.

Will saw the security guard walking up behind Mom.

"Is there a problem here, ma'am?"

"No problem as long as this man leaves the premises. The patient wants him to leave her alone." Mom cocked an eyebrow in Brian's direction. "Is there a problem with that, Mr. Montgomery?"

"I'll leave for now. You haven't seen the last of me though. Kate loves me. She'll want me back. You just wait and see." He looked over at Will. "If I can't have her, no one will."

The security guard crossed his arms, blocking the hallway to Katie's room. "It's time you left the premises, sir. As far as I'm concerned, you are not allowed in the hospital as long as Miss Winslow is here.

I can call Metro PD to remove you."

Brian poked Will in the chest. "You haven't seen the last of me."

Chapter 18

Surviving renovation …

Will headed home at Mom's urging. He went to Katie's house on the way there. Joe was locking up as Will pulled to the curb.

"Hey! How's Katie?" Joe reached out and clapped Will on the back when he reached the porch.

"She's in the trauma center. They're inducing a medical coma to bring down her blood pressure and help her heal." Will sighed. "She coded on the way in the ambulance, Joe." Will collapsed onto the porch swing.

"Are you okay?" Joe sat down beside him.

Will shook his head slowly. "No. Brian showed up making threats. I'm beginning to think he has some role in the odd things happening here, but I can't figure out how."

Joe nodded. "Want to see what we accomplished while you were driving back and forth to Nashville?"

Will stood. "Yes, I'd like some good news."

Joe stood and opened the front door. "I'm pretty happy with the work we did." He flipped on the lights.

"Oh, man, it looks amazing."

Fresh wallpaper, clean windows, gleaming woodwork, clean furniture. The wooden arch between the living room and the dining room looked spectacular.

"We vacuumed the furniture and carpet. The kitchen's been scrubbed down. The first floor is looking good." Joe opened the door to the kitchen to show Will. "I'll be back in the morning to paint trim in here."

"I don't know what to say. Thank you." Will sat down in a chair at the table and sobbed. "What if she doesn't ever wake up? What will I do without her?"

"Hey, bro. Everything will be okay. Why don't you come have dinner with Sally and me? She's frying chicken, your favorite." Joe lifted Will to his feet and embraced him. "I get it. She's your One. You won't be happy until she's home safe."

Will scrubbed the back of his hand across his face and nodded. "Thanks, Joe. If you're sure Sally's okay with me coming over."

"She's expecting you. Dad's already there." Joe laughed.

Will couldn't help but join him in laughter at the joke.

Kate opened her eyes to the glare of sunlight. Maddy was standing at the window with the curtains pulled back.

"Maddy?" Kate tried to move but found she couldn't do so easily. "What's going on?"

Maddy turned and slipped into the chair beside the bed. She took a tissue from the box on the tray to wipe away the tears streaming down her face. "These are happy tears. You've been asleep for two weeks. Well, in a medically induced coma. Welcome back."

"You haven't been here the whole two weeks, have you?"

"No, Billy and I been splitting the time. They told me last night they were lightening the sedation. It's so good to see your eyes, Katie."

"Am I better? Do I get to go home?"

A rap on the door prevented Maddy from replying. A nurse scurried in, checking vitals and such.

"Oh my!" She dropped her pen. "You're awake!" She bent over, picked up her pen, and hurried out into the hall.

"Do I look that bad?"

Maddy giggled. "Of course not. I guess they didn't expect you to be conscious until later. Billy will be in around nine to nine-thirty after he gets the work crew started."

"Work crew?"

"Maybe that was a secret." Maddy leaned forward. "Joe took a crew over to your house after you fell. When you came to Vanderbilt, a bunch of the guys decided to get involved fixing up your house. They got the first floor all gussied up. Billy's been supervising the volunteers before coming down to stay the daylight hours with you."

"He's been here every day?" Kate still felt groggy. "Think they'd add coffee to that IV drip. Then it'd be drip coffee, right?"

Maddy laughed. Then she laughed even harder.

The nurse entered followed by a doctor and a contingent of interns and residents.

"Kate Winslow, hard backward fall about one story almost three weeks ago. Fractured vertebrae. Concussion with loss of consciousness. resulting TBI expected." Interns scribbled furiously. "And conscious this morning due to a lightening of sedation overnight."

Kate looked up from her bed. "So, doctor, what's the prognosis? When can I get out of this bed and go home?"

"Also headstrong." The doctor turned to her, away from his students. "Do you understand just how lucky you are to survive that fall? And not be paralyzed?"

"Luck had nothing to do with it." Maddy crossed her arms. "God saved her in his strong arms."

Kate gave a short laugh. "What she said. I still need to get home to the renovation going on there. Even if I can't participate in it, I need to be there to give input."

He turned back to his students. "Clearly no memory or brain impairment. Course of treatment from here?"

Several students gave answers ranging from three months of rehab to just sending her home.

"I've thought long and hard on this, Miss Winslow. As long as people are around to help you, I'm thinking on sending you home in a back brace to keep any fragments from moving. It will allow the minute fractures to heal and allow you to go home. However, before that happens, I need to be sure you can walk the hallway end to end and go up and down the rehab stairs."

"Deal. When can I get out of the bed?" Kate was ready to go home now.

"As soon as the nurse has time to help you into a

back brace." The crowd of white coats turned and followed the doctor out of the room.

The nurse took her hand. "Soon, Katie. I'll get rehab up here with a back brace and some therapists to help you in and out of the bed. Then we'll see how much work you'll need to do to complete Dr. Turner's requirements."

"So, not as simple as it sounds." Kate sighed.

A rap on the door drew Kate's attention.

"Nothing ever is, in my experience." Will entered, a bright smile on his face. "You're awake. That's got to be a good sign."

Kate's heart flipped. "Will!"

"I'm here, Katie girl. I told you; wild horses couldn't drag me away." He came to her side and took her hand. "How do you feel?"

"Ready to go home, when they let me." Kate squeezed his hand. "I'm so glad to see you."

"Good to be seen. It's good to see your beautiful eyes." He looked as though he had more to say but chose to wait for another time.

Will moved over to Maddy and hugged her. He pulled an envelope from his pocket. "This came yesterday."

Maddy nodded. "What does it say?"

"Yes."

Maddy shrieked and hugged him tightly. "Congratulations, Billy!"

"What is it?"

"A job offer. At an engineering firm not far from here. It's a great offer."

Even though Will was smiling, Kate's heart sank. *A job? In Nashville? What will that do to our chances for a long-term relationship?*

"Never fear. I don't find a thirty-minute drive a bad commute to maintain a home in Adams. Too many reasons to stay in my hometown." He winked at her. "And I'll have a steady income." His eyes communicated more than his words implied.

Kate tried to smile. "When do you start?"

"I made it clear that I needed you to go home from here before I'd start work." He sat in the chair Maddy had vacated and grabbed Kate's hand. "I promised to be by your side as long as you're in the hospital. They understood. I'd have turned them down if they hadn't."

Maddy picked up her tote bag and stuffed her Bible and books into it. "I'll head on home then. Katie, you work on the rehab requirement so you can come home."

Home. For the first time in a long time, I have somewhere to go home with people who care about me. Tears leaked down the sides of her face onto her pillow.

Will pulled out his pocket handkerchief and wiped them away. "Are you in pain? Do I need to get the nurse?"

"No, it's just so good to have family who care about me and want me with them."

"Here I thought you were just sad to see me leave." Maddy laughed. "I'll go home and prepare the guest room for you. Until you're well enough, I'll have no arguments to the contrary."

Kate nodded. "Yes, ma'am."

Maddy kissed Will and waved good-bye to Kate.

After she left, Will kissed the hand he held. "I now have a full-time job. I don't have to live with my parents anymore. Do you know what that means?"

Kate shook her head slowly. "Sorry, I've been asleep for two weeks. I'm not very quick on the uptake."

"You know how I feel. I think you feel the same way. I can support us now."

"No, don't say it, Will. I can't agree to any long-term commitments after being sedated for so long. You know how it is for concussions and sedation. I'm not supposed to sign any contracts or agree to buy anything for twenty-four hours. I don't want to tell you 'No.'" She squeezed his hand to reassure him. "Please wait to say what I think you're going to say."

His bright eyes clouded. "We have a future together, even if you can't agree to it now. I'm not going away." He reached down with the other hand to a bulge in his jeans pocket.

143

Chapter 19

Engaging life goals …

Kate gasped as Will pulled something out of his jeans pocket. "I took your phone home with me while you were unconscious."

She sighed. Kate feared he had an engagement ring in that pocket. Yet, what if he did? She'd danced an imaginary wedding waltz with him before falling down that shaft. Still, she had a long recovery ahead of her. Her reasons for avoiding that question were sound. Weren't they?

"Will, are you okay?" She squeezed his hand. "Everything between us is still all right, isn't it?"

He flashed a crooked smile. "As long as we're together, my friend."

A rap at the door revealed a physical therapist with a back brace for Kate. Will stepped into the hall while the therapist helped her out of bed and fit the brace to her body. When he left, Will came back into the room where Kate was sitting in a chair.

Will pulled a chair up beside her. "I'm so glad to see you upright."

"The view's a lot better from here." She felt her

heart race. "Thank you for spending so much time at my side. I know that can be torturous. I sat at the bedside of both my parents and my great aunt, watching them each die."

"I had it better because I wasn't going to let you die." Will took her hand. "I'm not going away."

Kate squeezed his hand. "I'm holding you to that promise."

Two therapists entered the room, one with a walker, the other wearing a gait belt like a bandolier.

"Kate, I'm Doug and this is Marcie. Are you ready to see what's happening outside of these four walls?"

"Yes, please." Kate tried to stand on her own, then she fell back into the chair.

"Whoa!" Doug rushed over to her with the walker. "We have things to make that safer until you get stronger. You want to avoid falling again."

Marcie looped the gait belt around Kate. "Okay, try that again. Don't reach for the walker until you've stood up."

Doug took hold of the gait belt and kept it taut as Marcie helped her navigate the walker.

Will clapped as she stood up. "There's my girl!"

Pain shot down her spine into her legs. "So much pain."

"Gonna have to push through it." Doug tightened his grip on the gait belt.

Marcie grabbed Kate's IV pole. "We'll just walk out to the hall. We can return to your room when the pain gets unbearable. Okay?"

Kate took a deep breath and stood as straight as she could. "Let's do this."

Will stood with her. "I believe in you, Katie. You

can do this and come home."

She nodded, but pain shot into her neck and head. *Must keep going to get out of here. Will needs to start his adult job soon. Maybe then, we can make plans.*

Will tagged along behind her. She wished he couldn't see her this way.

"Good job, Miss Kate. You're doing well." Marcie led Kate to the rehab steps and took the walker away.

Kate took a deep breath. Then she walked up the two steps, crossed the platform, and descended the steps on the other side.

"Great job!" Doug still held the gait belt to catch her if she should fall. "How are you feeling?"

"Tired and in pain." Kate was out of breath for such a short walk.

"You are one lucky girl." Marcie handed the walker back to her. "Let's go on back to your room. We can remove the back brace and let you take a nap."

Kate pushed the walker back to her room with little need for help. *God was watching out for me; no permanent damage, and I can go home soon.*

At the start of the next week, Will began his job at a big civil engineering firm in Nashville. He battled the rush hour traffic in the morning and was late on his first day. Now he experienced trying to come home in traffic. *Is this worth a paycheck? Sitting in front of a computer all day is not who I am. I need to be working with my hands, being outside in the sunshine, carrying out the civil engineer plans.*

He parked in front of his parents' house and pulled loose the tie he'd worn for apparently no good reason. *What should I do? If I want to marry Katie, I need a steady income, especially while she's getting the B&B up and running.* At least Katie was home from the hospital. He stepped out of his truck.

"Will!"

Katie's call from the porch reinvigorated him. He hurried up the walk and took the steps to the porch by twos. He hugged her, and her back brace, carefully.

"How's your day been, sweet girl?" Will refrained from kissing her even though it was all he wanted to do. "I filled out paperwork all day."

"Joe took me over to the house for a time. They've done such a great job! The second floor is almost done as well. They found another door into the inner sanctum in the wall of my bedroom. It looks like every floor has access to the safe room. My question is 'How did the intruder get into the sanctum without the doors being revealed?'"

"Good question." Will shook his head. "We're obviously missing something important."

"Let's go to the house after dinner and check it out, if you think my back brace will fit in the passageway."

"Dinner's ready!" Maddy's voice carried out onto the front porch.

"Maddy's making chili, but I saw her putting spaghetti in it." Katie looked confused.

Will laughed. "Mom's from Kentucky near Cincinnati. Ever heard of Skyline Chili? It has spaghetti in it, even chocolate. Just wait until she makes spaghetti."

Katie slipped under Will's arm as he held the door

for her. "Why?"

"Same recipe as the chili, only thicker, with beans, over spaghetti."

Kate giggled. "Truly? Are you pulling my leg?"

Will whispered in her ear. "She adds chili beans to her spaghetti sauce. Her chili is the same as the spaghetti, just watered down. Spaghetti one day, chili the next."

Katie snorted trying to hold in the laughter building in her chest. Her silent laughter shook her body.

"I wouldn't kid about Mom's cooking." Will gave a short laugh. "I'm not complaining about it."

When they entered the kitchen, Maddy was placing the Dutch oven on the table. A big bowl of oyster crackers sat beside it. "What are you two giggling about?"

Katie laughed outright then.

Will couldn't contain his laughter either. "Skyline chili, Mom. We were talking about Skyline chili."

Katie started a fresh round of laughter as she settled in her chair.

"You two worry me sometimes. It's like the two of you live in a different world than the rest of us. Like twins who speak their own language."

"Who's having twins?" Dad entered the room and slipped into his chair.

Will looked at Katie, and they laughed even harder.

Maddy laughed then. "No one is having twins, Porter."

"So, pass the chili this way."

A fresh round of laughter struck Will and Katie at

the word "chili." Katie was gasping for breath. Will thought they might never stop laughing, for the rest of their lives, together. He took her hand in his under the table. She squeezed it, like a promise for the future.

After dinner, Kate and Will took his truck to the future B&B.

Kate unlocked the door and flipped on the lights. "It looks so amazing. Joe and his friends did such a great job. Look at this."

She hurried as best she could to the alcove where the first-floor door was located. "Look how they matched the wallpaper on the door to the wall, so it blends in." Kate pushed the button, and the door swung open. "If you didn't know it was here, you'd never notice it."

Will shined his flashlight down the dark passageway. He took a deep breath. "Every time we enter this space, one of us gets hurt. Promise me you won't take any unnecessary risks."

"Trust me. This back brace will keep me from doing too much." Kate took his hand. "I promise. That goes for you too."

Will nodded. He took her hand. "Ready for another adventure?"

"As long as it's with you." She gazed into his dark eyes.

He smiled. "Let's go." Will entered the passage with Kate behind him.

Chapter 20

Discovering passages …

Instead of the framing Kate expected to find, the walls inside the passage were finished and painted. The floors were hardwood covered in the dust of being forgotten for over a century. Sconces on the walls held melted candlewax from days before electricity. How could an electrician wire the house without finding this passage? However, it did explain why she had no outlets on the passage wall in her bedroom.

Will tightened his grip on her hand as they reached the end of the passage.

A narrow stairwell rose before them with a set of stairs to the second floor, and a set went down to the cellar. The hall continued past the stairs to another door with light coming in around it.

Will turned to face Kate. "Where does that come out?"

"Maybe the kitchen. Perhaps these halls were used by the serving staff."

"That makes sense. Once there was no staff, your ancestors covered it over to protect the secret safe room." Will leaned against the wall.

"You know what this means, don't you?" Kate gasped. "Someone can get into the house from the root cellar."

"Every time I've scouted around the house, a padlock has been on the cellar doors. I didn't have a key to the lock. Do you?"

Will faced her in the light of the flashlight. His eyes gleamed and sparkled with love. Kate's cheeks warmed. *I love him, of course. But how can I marry him with this house and its mysteries hanging over my head? How long will he be glad to drive the trip to Nashville every workday?*

"Katie, are you with me?" Will's eyes reflected worry now. "Did I lose you there?"

She shook her head. "No. I don't have another key."

"Now that I think on it, that lock was quite new looking."

"Are you saying someone replaced the lock, and they alone have the key?" Kate shivered though the passage was warm. "If that's so, we need to cut the lock off and replace it with a new one that we alone have the key."

Will examined the door. "Yes, someone's been through the door recently. See the scuffs and footprints in the dust?"

"That means someone could be on the other side of my bedroom wall." Fear caused Kate to tense; pain radiated from her back. "Who would do such a thing to me?"

"Well, someone with footprints, not a spiritual being." Will threw the bolt on the door to the cellar. "That may not keep someone from breaking the door open."

"It's better than being easily accessible." Kate's voice squeaked out a whisper. "We need that new padlock yesterday."

Will unlocked the bolt. "On second thought, I want to see how the passageway works from the root cellar. I can go over to Dad's store and get a new padlock tonight." Will put an arm around her and squeezed gently. "You're shaking. Are you okay?"

"No. Let's go get the padlock and secure the root cellar." Kate laid her head on his shoulder. "We can explore more tomorrow."

Kate turned and slid back to the alcove door. Will closed it after they were out.

"I'll go to the store and pick up a lock. Why don't you stay here and rest while I'm gone?" Will touched her arm. "Will you be okay?"

Kate nodded. He had taken her response to his almost proposal hard. While his eyes said he loved her still, he had stopped giving frequent hugs, and kisses were rare. *I guess I got what I asked for. Sometimes what we want isn't what we really need.* She longed for his touch.

After Will slammed the front door closed, Kate took the stairs to her bedroom. As she entered, she was consumed by the transformation of the master bedroom. Damask stripes with roses. New mauve curtains? Maddy must have found time for that. A matching duvet on the bed brought the room together. The wallpaper blended perfectly with the door into the passageway.

Kate stared at the door. *Should I go in alone? It couldn't hurt to just look, could it?* She found the entry button, and the door popped open. Using the flashlight on her phone, she peered into the passageway. Like the downstairs, the floor and walls were finished and dusty. But the dust on the floor had been scuffed by the intruder. *Is that where the voices came from? Someone outside my bedroom?*

She wasn't going exploring when she was there by herself, so Kate pulled the door closed. She didn't even know how to open the door from inside the passage. She'd watched way too many *Scooby-Doo*s to have someone close the door on her, trapping her in the walls.

Kate removed her back brace and with great care lay on top of the duvet. A mauve book on the nightstand caught her eye. She stretched and nabbed it.

A Bible that matched the duvet. Another Maddy gift no doubt. When she opened the book, she saw an inscription:

To my dear Katie,

> *You've always been like the daughter I never had. Let the Lord carry your burdens. Lean on Him to care for you. Reach out to the people who love you best.*
> *All my love, Maddy Bell.*

Kate smiled. *Maybe one day I'll be legally connected as a daughter-in-law.* Even though it didn't say so, Maddy implied that she'd marry Will. Right now, though, it seemed hard to see past tonight.

She must have drifted off because suddenly she heard a knock at her bedroom door in the wall.

"You there, Katie?" Will's deep voice. "Can I enter?"

Kate moved to sitting on the edge of the bed. "Yes,

if you know how to work it." She strapped the back brace back in place.

Before she could get to the wall to let Will in, the door popped open. Will stepped out with cobwebs in his hair and dust on his clothes.

"I cut off the padlock and decided to see how the passage works from the cellar."

Kate felt a stab in her heart. "You took an adventure without me?"

"The steps are treacherous. They need rails and renovation as well. You don't need to be on them while you're in a back brace." Will sat beside her on the bed. "We'll have more adventures, Katie. This was merely a security event. I just wanted to see if whoever it was could get to your bedroom and get in."

Kate clasped his hand. "And the answer is yes, he can."

"Or she can." Will added. "Let's head back to Mom and Dad's for dessert. I noticed a chocolate cake in the fridge when I was helping Mom clean up from our dinner. A slice right now sounds awfully good."

Will stood and helped Kate up. "Here's a key to the new padlock. I'll keep one on my ring of your keys. Let's go lock up the cellar."

Kate and Will turned off lights, made sure the front door was locked then went out the back door at the kitchen. Not far from the back stairs, the cellar doors gaped open. A broken padlock lay nearby.

"I didn't even think to check the root cellar. I assumed it was its own thing, under the house but not part of it."

Will laughed. "I found the screens down there. I also found something else that's disturbing."

"What?" Kate put her hand on his arm. *What else could go wrong?*

"A cot, a blanket, snacks, and clothing." Will took her hand. "It looks like someone has been living there."

Chapter 21

Root cellar squatter …

Kate grabbed Will's arm. "Someone's camping in my root cellar? Who?"

"I don't know. Maybe we should give Andy a call for fingerprint analysis or something. I placed one of those wildlife cameras in the bush to capture a picture of the squatter. Smile for the camera, Katie."

"In this back brace, no thank you. I'm ready to go back to your house now. Should we lock it up or leave it open?"

"I'm calling Andy to come over and bring the forensic team." Will stroked his chin. "Then I think we lock it up. We don't need vandalism again."

Kate wanted to stroke his dark stubble, too, but she held back. *I need to heal before I can fall into another relationship.*

Will called the Robertson County Sheriff's Department. "Hi, is Andy available?" He looked at her. "Elevator music. They're getting him to the phone."

Kate nodded carefully then sat in one of the old lawn chairs on the patio. "We need to spruce up out here too. And rip out all of the garden." She sighed. *So much to do. Will I survive it? Will doesn't have time to deal with this mess now that he's working in Nashville.*

"Andy! We've found evidence of the person getting into the house. They've been squatting in the root cellar. … Right. The root cellar has access to an internal passageway in the house. Thought you'd like to bring your forensic team over. … Great. I'll be here after I take Katie back to the house." Will clicked off and put his phone in his jeans pocket. "Come on, let's get you back to Mom and Dad's. I'll come back and deal with the police."

Will closed the root cellar doors, then he and Kate walked around front to his truck.

"Thank you. I wish I could stay, but I'm just not strong enough now." *Useless, that's how I feel.*

"You're making great strides. You were able to come out here tonight. You're able to walk and take the steps. You don't need the walker to get around."

He held the door open and helped her into his truck. The touch of his hand on hers sizzled. *Did he feel that too?*

A few minutes later, they arrived back at Will's house. He helped her down from the truck cab and walked with her to the front door of his parents' home. "I'll be back when the sheriff's crew is finished with forensics. You should go on to bed. I'll save you a slice of that chocolate cake."

Kate held his arm longer than usual. "I don't know what to say."

"Next time I almost ask, say yes." Will winked and kissed her cheek. "I'll be back as soon as I can." He squeezed her hand and headed back into the dark night.

The truck headlights swept over the house as he

backed out of the driveway. Crickets and tree frogs sang in the dark. Fireflies flashed randomly across the yard. She shivered in the damp summer evening. *So different from living in Nashville.*

Will shifted from Reverse to Drive and glanced at the porch. Katie still stood there with her arms wrapped around that back brace. He hated to leave her there, but Mom and Dad would take good care of her while he pursued the person responsible for the mayhem at Katie's house. He drove the short distance to her house and arrived just as the Robertson County Sheriff's vehicles pulled up in front. Will jumped out to greet them.

"Andy, thanks for coming so quickly." They shook hands.

The remaining vehicles discharged other officers with forensic cases and white coveralls to pull on. Will led the way to the root cellar and showed them the door to the cellar and shared what he knew about what they'd find down in the dark.

One man bagged the cut lock. Another dusted for prints on the door and on the ladder steps. Someone else bagged the pillowcase on the cot, another the coffee mug beside it.

Meanwhile Andy asked questions. "When did you discover the squatter's items?"

"Today, this evening." Will tried to remember what time. "After dinner."

"Why'd you cut off the lock? Did you check with

Kate first?"

"Yes, she didn't have a key to the lock." Will rubbed his neck. It had been a long day. He'd have to get up and do it all again tomorrow. "I'm weary, Andy. I'm working full time in Nashville now. Any way this questioning can be over? I have no idea who's been in the cellar. I just don't want them back any time soon."

"Sure. How's Katie doing?" Andy put away his notepad and pen. "Are we thinking this same person is responsible for yours and Katie's injuries?"

Will shrugged. "Who knows? It's possible."

"Don't guess the Bell Witch needs a cot or coffee." Andy raised an eyebrow.

"I wouldn't think so." Will rolled his eyes. "Please don't start that line of thought with Katie. She thinks she's hearing voices. She's been traumatized too much without starting that line of questioning."

"Voices?"

"Don't think she backed herself down that hatch. I know she didn't vandalize the house or throw paint on her car." Will rubbed his neck. "And I'm the one who knocked her over on the ladder and broke her arm."

"You have to admit, she's taken a lot of punishment due to something going on." Andy thumped Will's back. "Try to relax. I'm just asking questions no one may have asked yet. Trying to tie all this misfortune together."

Will nodded. "I get that, but you know Katie is special to me. I don't want her hurt anymore."

A man in uniform approached Andy. "Sir, we've got the most likely items secured and lifted prints."

"Head back to the lab with the evidence. Then you can go back to the station."

Will crossed his arms. "How long until you find something?"

Andy shrugged. "Depends on whether the person is in the system or not. If not, we'll need to start beating the bushes for suspects to match the DNA and fingerprints."

"Make sure you test Brian Montgomery. My gut says he's involved, though I'm not sure how." Will sank into a patio chair.

"I know why. He's competition for the girl you've loved your whole life. Don't have to be much of a detective to know that." Andy laughed. "We'll finish up here. Have you got a new lock for the door?"

Will pulled the padlock from his pocket and handed it to Andy.

"You've got the key?" Andy took it from him.

"Got it. Katie has the second key."

"Go home and get some rest. And congrats on the new job." Andy affixed the padlock to the door.

Will walked out to the front curb with Andy and the forensic team. He counted the people as they entered vehicles. He sure didn't want someone slipping back into the house for tonight.

Would this ever end?

161

Chapter 22

Return of the voices …

Kate slipped into the bed, pulling the covers over her as she lay down. Sitting up in bed to get the cover wasn't doable yet. Random thoughts came into her brain as she tried to fall asleep. Her back throbbed. Will hadn't come home yet. Was the house worth the pain and cost of renovating?

That's when the voice began again.

"Why do you want to live in Adams? … Is it worth the aggravation and injury? … You know you are a target for injury. … You don't want to die over this house, do you?"

Kate jerked awake, screaming. *A dream?*

The door to the room opened. Will's head appeared. "Everything okay, Katie?"

"Will is losing interest in you, Kate. … You're going to grow old alone in Adams." The real voice was smooth and melodic.

"Shh. Listen." Kate waved him in. The voice was real. She wasn't imagining it.

Will nodded and came in. He sat in a chair near the door.

Kate called out to the disembodied voice. "Who are you? Why are you saying these things? How are you doing this?"

"Will's driving to Nashville. ... Brian never wanted to do that. ... How long do you think he will want to do it?" The voice taunted her.

"How do you know about Brian?" Kate shook her head at Will who looked as though he'd skyrocket through the ceiling.

"I thought you'd read the books and did the research, Kate."

"Are you trying to say you're the Bell Witch?" Kate wasn't sure what to say next now that Will could hear it too.

Will moved closer to the bed, listening to the voice. He poked around the nightstand until he saw the light from her cellphone. He picked it up and handed it to her.

She stared into the screen. Instant Messenger was open.

The voice started again. "Brian loved you. ... He'd take you back. ... Will is a bad choice, Kate."

"Brian?" Kate's blood boiled through her. "How dare you! Do not call me on Instant Messenger again. You are blocked." She opened the app and blocked his account.

"I didn't know that was possible. How did he do that?" Will took the phone from her and placed it on the nightstand.

"It's happened to me before. I was trading messages with someone when suddenly I heard her voice. She was able to connect, somehow." Kate sighed. "How dare he create so much fear in me? I thought I was losing my mind."

"One mystery solved. The police are checking fingerprints and eventually DNA from the root cellar. Perhaps we'll know more tomorrow. Good night, Katie." Will slipped from the room and pulled the door closed.

Will stepped into his own room. *How dare the man treat Katie like that?* He took off his shoe and threw it into the closet. He took off the other and threw it as well.

"Billy!" Mom's voice. "Whatever your problem is, some of us are trying to sleep."

A rap on his door startled him. "Are you decent, son?"

"Come in, Mom."

The door opened, and she stepped in. She ran a finger along his chest of drawers. Then she closed the two drawers that were hanging open. "Really, Billy. You should keep your room neater. You asked me not to clean in here after you graduated."

"What do you want, Mom?" Will cleared his strewn clothes from a chair, so she could sit. "I heard the voice Katie has been hearing. It was Brian transmitting through a phone app."

"How dare he?" Mom sat, then she stood again. "How dare he!"

"Exactly why I threw the shoes. I'm sorry I kept you up." Will leaned against the chest of drawers.

Mom stood and retied the sash on her robe. "I'm

going back downstairs."

"Thought you were going to bed, Mom."

"I'm so riled up now; I couldn't sleep. I need to bake something." She kissed his cheek and ruffled his hair. "I know you are a better man than that Brian is. Take care of our Katie."

Will gave her a smile. "You know I will."

When Will entered the kitchen, he expected to see Mom. Instead, it was Katie in a robe, cutting a coffee cake and pouring coffee.

"Don't you look nice." Katie gave him a wide grin. "Don't create heart-throbbing all over your office in those smart dress pants and shirt. Should you have a tie?"

"I wore one yesterday. No one else does, though I think they keep a generic one on the hook behind their office doors." He sat down as Katie brought over his cup of coffee.

"Your mom stuck her head in my room early. She'd started the coffee and had the coffeecake she made in the wee hours in the oven reheating. She went back to bed." Katie set a place for herself and for Dad. "Why was she up in the night baking?"

"I told her about Brian's trick. She was upset. When she's upset, she bakes."

Dad entered the kitchen. "I hear we have tag-team breakfast today. To whom do we owe Maddy's baking?" He scooted out the chair as Katie set his coffee at his place.

"Brian." Will and Katie spoke at the same time.

Dad laughed. "At least you both agree. What did that boy do now?"

Will ate while Katie explained how Brian had used an app on her phone to send verbal messages to her, even cause her fall down the shaft.

"You need a restraining order, Katie girl. Go by the sheriff's office and file one. This man is a hazard you don't need in your life, you hear me?"

"Yes, sir, Uncle Porter." Katie nodded and slipped into a chair as best as she could in a back brace. "This sour cream coffee cake is fantastic. It may be the best thing Brian has ever caused by his behavior."

Will and Dad both laughed.

Will jumped up. "I better get going. I got stuck in traffic yesterday and was late." He picked up his leather satchel and peeked inside. "Did Mom make this lunch too?"

"No, I did." Katie walked with him to the front door. "Think of me when you have lunch. Your dad's taking me over to the house to direct whatever work crew shows up today."

Will leaned in and kissed her. "I'll see you there later."

Katie's cheeks reddened. "Can't wait."

Kate returned to the table.

"Billy would never treat you like that ex-boyfriend of yours."

She nodded carefully. "I know that. Will's better in all regards. Someday Brian may be famous, but I won't take the abuse he hands out anymore. And I won't lie when the reporters come asking what it was like to have Brian Montgomery as a boyfriend."

"When you say abuse, exactly what are you talking about?" Maddy had entered the kitchen, startling both Kate and Uncle Porter.

"Not out and out physical abuse." Kate folded her napkin twice then reopened it. "Whatever happened, it was always due to something I had done. If he'd lost something, it was always going to be my fault, somehow. If I was late, it ruined the evening. Even getting turned down by a record company, he thought I had sabotaged him."

"Verbal abuse is still abuse, Katie girl." Uncle Porter rose from the table. "When you're ready, we'll go by the sheriff's before going to your house."

"Okay." Kate stood and headed upstairs slowly.

Chapter 23

The butler in the pantry with the candlestick …

After Kate took out a restraining order against Brian, Uncle Porter drove her to the house. No one seemed to be around that morning. That was okay. She could use some time alone to ponder the mysteries in her life, not only the ones in the house. She placed her laptop on the dining table, connected to her Wi-Fi, and opened Word. She titled the new document "Things Needed to Run a B&B."

The first section she titled, "Linens." The next was "Bedroom accessories" then "Bathroom accoutrements." Finally, she added, "Menu options."

"Not exactly what you can pick up from Amazon." She muttered to herself as she added "Patio & garden" and listed bistro sets, lawn chairs, and garden tools. "Won't need any of that before next spring at the rate we're moving." Kate sat staring at the computer screen, but she wasn't moved to complete her lists.

Kate closed the laptop and picked up her dust mop and duster. She popped open the door in the alcove to the passageway and used a wallpaper sampler book to prop it open, so she wouldn't be trapped inside. She made sure she had her cell phone and air pods. Setting a lantern at the entrance, she went to work cleaning the passageway: dusting the polished wood floor and the walls and ridding the cobwebs from the ceiling. She also removed the ancient candles and wax drippings from the sconces.

She reached the juncture of the narrow stairs to the second floor and to the root cellar. Without light in the cellar, Kate couldn't see the evidence of an unknown squatter. She shivered. *It could be anyone. Brian? A homeless person? An evil crime boss?* She laughed. *A root cellar was not usually an evil lair.* Nevertheless, Kate pulled the door to the cellar closed and threw the antique bolt lock into place. *Perhaps we should install another lock as well.*

At the mysterious extra door just past the stairwell landing, Kate found the sconce holding a used candle wasn't straight. She pulled the used taper from the base and realized the sconce itself moved. None of the others had moved. She grabbed the base and pulled and pushed on the sconce. She was nearly out of strength from cleaning in a back brace when Kate shoved a different direction, and the sconce moved, but so did the extra door. It opened creaking and a fog of dust plumed into the passageway revealing a storage room full of cobwebs and dust. It looked as though no one had been in there in one hundred years.

Preserves, chutneys, and pickles in Mason jars graced one set of shelves. Preserved green beans, lima beans, and tomatoes filled another. Another shelf held jars of dried beans, seeds, and popcorn kernels. *Not sure how much of this is edible after one hundred years.* But if this was a butler's pantry, surely, he didn't need to enter the passage to get to it. Kate cleaned and poked around in the small room. The last shelf held old cookbooks and recipe tins full to overflowing with paper scraps. She reached back into the shelf and found a lever. When she pulled it down, the shelf rotated out into the kitchen from inside the pantry. *Just wait until Will sees this!*

Kate began removing old food from the pantry shelves. Everything was wildly out of date. She'd need Will to carry the trash bag to the alley. The pantry in the kitchen stretched across one wall of the room. It was shallow but wide with grooved wood panel doors with clicky knobs to open and latch. With part of the shelf unit moving to display the butler's pantry, the space was phenomenal. *Had Aunt Katharine known about it? She'd have used it all for some of the family get-togethers at this house if she had.*

By lunchtime, Kate was tired and in pain. She had done way more than she had planned or that she should have done. Despite the pain, she was excited about her discovery and the pantry clean out. She munched on some baby carrots, fixed a ham sandwich from the fridge, and drank a Coke, of course. Then she took medication and went upstairs to lie down.

Kate woke to a pounding sound coming from the backyard. She rose as quickly as possible and put on the back brace. She carefully descended the creaky steps and hurried through the kitchen to the back door.

A blonde woman was kicking the root cellar doors and shouting curses.

"Can I help you?" Kate stayed at the top of the steps wanting to avoid direct confrontation with the angry woman.

The woman looked up to her. She was tall, slim, and model beautiful beneath the grime of homelessness. And she was angry.

"What happened to my lock? You have no right to take it off." Her accent was pure Georgian southern belle. "I bought that lock. Now it's gone."

"Sorry, but this is my house, including the root cellar. Are you the person who's been staying there?"

"So, you're the infamous Kate Winslow the town is talking about. Everyone wants to help poor Katie establish her bed and breakfast. They're also talking about you and Will, and you and Andy, and you and Terrance, too. You may be the flavor of the month, Miss Kate, but Will is mine. He'll remember that long before you can have him under your spell, witch."

Kate blinked at the vitriol spewing from the beautiful blonde. That she called her a witch said more than the blonde thought she'd said. Kate remembered the "Bell Witch" on her garage door and on the back of the front entry door. Paint on the car? Not out of the realm of possibility with her temper.

"I need to ask you to leave, ma'am. I didn't catch your name."

"Viola Chastain. You just ask Will who I am. He'll tell you." She kicked the root cellar door again, smoothed back her hair, and waltzed out the gate to the front.

Kate's phone buzzed with a notification. She glanced at it, nothing big, but since the phone was in her hand, she called Andy. "Officer Andy Lawrence, please."

When Andy pulled up out front, Kate was on the porch swing. He ran up the front yard.

"Are you okay, Katie?"

"Yes, but I know who has been camping in my cellar. She was just here having a hissy fit about the lock on the root cellar doors being changed."

Andy sunk down onto the porch steps. "Viola Chastain. Having a hissy fit is a perfect description. Did she try to hurt you?"

"Not physically. She called me a witch." A laugh bubbled up inside. "A witch. Can you believe it?" She tried not to laugh because it hurt, but she lost the struggle.

Andy nodded. "You'll love the rest of the story. She called the sheriff's office wanting to swear out a complaint against you for denying her access to her stuff in your root cellar."

Kate strangled on a laugh. "What happened?"

"An officer met her at Adams Station BBQ and arrested her. She's in a cell at the moment." Andy laughed as well. "We'll check her fingerprints and DNA, but she's essentially confessed to being in your root cellar. Did she deck Will with a crowbar? Did she make you fall down the shaft from the attic? The list may grow from only trespass."

"I guess my call is superfluous. It's okay. I just wanted you to know what was happening. Viola surprised me."

Andy took Kate's hand. "It's what Viola excels at. She wasn't always homeless. I'm just glad she didn't hurt you." He released her hand. "Sorry. That was awkward. I know you and Will are a thing. That's what's wrong with Viola. She believed that Will would eventually be hers. Then you showed up, crushing her long-term plans. That made her desperate."

"I didn't know anything about her. Will nor Maddy or Porter have even mentioned her. No wonder she's hurt."

"That's not your fault, Kate. All you did was inherit a house and reacquaint with your childhood flame. Viola's in the wrong here, not you." Andy patted her arm. "We'll take care of it."

"Okay." Kate shook her head. "I just feel bad for her."

"That's because you're kind. I'll work up the complaint paperwork and swing by tomorrow for you to sign it." Andy stood and stretched. "See you later."

"Thanks." She waved as he drove off. Then she had an idea and whipped out her phone. "Hello, Maddy? Could you go to the grocery for me? Will and I need to have a heart-to-heart talk about Viola Chastain."

Chapter 24

Telling the story of Viola Chastain …

Will pulled up under the old trees at the curb of 415 Spring Street. He looked up at the house as he stepped away from the curb. *We need to hire painters.*

He found a box from Restorers.com on the porch. He picked it up to bring in. *Heavy, must be the locks for the bedroom doors.* Will used his key to enter the house.

The smell of dinner cooking whetted his appetite. *Has Mom been here?* Will put the box on the bottom step for now. He wandered into the kitchen to find Kate sitting at the table. "Good afternoon. It smells amazing in here." He reached a hand into the chopped vegetable platter and snagged a carrot.

"Beef stew, cornbread, veggies, and cake."

"Wow! You've been busy." He crunched the carrot. "How's your back? That's a lot of standing in the kitchen."

"Your mom helped by going to the store for groceries and then retrieving my mixer, pressure cooker, and kitchen supplies box from the garage." Katie smiled. "I also sat to do all the chopping and mixing."

"What's the occasion?" Will sat down across the table. "Did I miss your birthday?"

"No, silly. Don't you remember we used to celebrate my half birthday every July since my real birthday is in January? We never saw each other in January, all these years we've known each other." She sighed. "We need the opportunity to talk about our lives apart from one another. That's hard to do at your parents' dinner table."

Will's heart clenched. *Is she breaking up with me? Does she not want to see me anymore? What have I done?* "Is everything okay?"

"Found a butler's pantry inside the wall today. Also found out who's been sleeping in the root cellar. A pretty profound day all around."

The pressure cooker beeped, and Kate rose to tend to it. She opened the cooker and spooned stew into each bowl.

"You went in the passage without backup?" Once it was out of his mouth, he knew just how ridiculous it sounded. "I mean you went in alone. You should have waited for me."

Katie shrugged and grimaced. "It was fine. I propped open the door and shined the lantern down the passage. I was just cleaning the dust off the floor and walls."

"You're in pain. Can I finish the meal?" That sinking feeling in his gut wasn't hunger. Something was wrong.

"No, it's finished. You can carry it to the table."

She handed him a basket of corn muffins and a butter dish. Then he carried bowls of stew to the table.

She brought the cake, then two small plates. Utensils and iced tea were already on the table.

Katie took his hand. "Would you pray over the meal?"

He nodded. "Lord, thank you for your watch care over us today and always. Keep us in your will and use this food to nourish, heal, and strengthen us for your service. Amen."

Katie dipped her spoon into the stew, blew on it, and took a bite. "Hmm. Does it need salt?"

Will put the whole spoonful in his mouth. *Too hot.* He couldn't taste it because his tongue was singed. After chewing carefully, he swallowed as soon as he could. "It tastes fine to me. Just pretty hot." He took a muffin and buttered it. "What's going on, Katie?"

"I had a surprise visitor today. One I hadn't met nor heard of before this afternoon." She also took a corn muffin and buttered it. "This person was quite angry because the new lock had been placed on the cellar doors. Said person went to the sheriff's to swear out a complaint against me for not allowing her to get her things."

"Her?" Will choked on a bite of muffin. He coughed and sputtered. Once he drank a bit of tea, the cough subsided. "Her? I was sure it was Brian."

"Yes, she's in a cell for criminal trespass by her own admission. She seems to think I've stolen someone from her." Katie ate another bite of stew. "That you and she were to get married once you had a real job."

"Viola Chastain?" Will's stomach turned. "I am not in love with Viola. She made promises to herself."

"That's not the way she tells it. And she's drop dead gorgeous."

"Beauty is as beauty does."

"Will! That is not a kind thing to say about anyone." Katie put down her spoon. "We both had a life prior to my move back here. If you're promised to Viola, you need to either keep the promise or let her know what your intentions are. That's the only gentleman thing to do."

"Criminal trespass. Possibly assault! How can you take her side?"

Katie folded her napkin and placed it on the table. "Someone must be on her side. Why not me?"

"Don't you see? Every man in town wanted to date her, but in a couple of dates every man knew she was … well … deranged."

"Oh, Will…" Katie crossed her arms.

"You saw her! She blamed you for locking your own root cellar, so she couldn't get in. Isn't that just a little over the edge?"

"Perhaps, but she still needs consideration. I cannot in good conscience move forward in our relationship until all others are resolved. Is that irrational too?"

Will crossed his arms. "No. I see what you are saying, but more contact with Viola breeds more irrational contact with Viola. It's a no-win situation."

"She thinks I'm scooping up all the available men in Adams, like I'm casting spells over them like a witch, like Kate the Bell Witch! She even called me that."

Katie looked like she could cry.

Warning, Will! Irrational woman event! Step carefully around this or you could lose her trust. Watch the words coming out of your mouth!

"Katie, you are not a witch. You are not casting spells or scooping up men. If men are bewitched, it's by your goodness and kindness. I've only had eyes for you most of my life." Will opened his arms and came toward her. "I'm not the enemy here. Are we okay?"

Katie sniffed and wiped her cheeks where her tears had escaped. As Katie moved toward his open arms, a mournful Banshee shriek issued from the walls.

"AIEEEEE!"

Chapter 25

When the walls cry out …

Will's heart jumped. "What was that?"

"I'm calling 911!" Katie collapsed into a chair and grabbed her phone.

Will ran to the alcove access and opened the door. He heard footsteps running away from him, echoing in the enclosed space. When he reached the door to the cellar, the latch was broken, and the door was splintered. *Could Viola do such a thing?*

Will descended to the cellar and raced up the steep ladder-like stairs to the backyard. He saw a figure escaping through the gate to the front yard. "Stop!"

A siren split the summer evening noises followed by the appearance of flashing lights. The sheriff's car leapt over the curb into the yard blocking the runner's path. Long blonde hair flew into the intruder's face as she fell over the hood of the car.

Andy jumped out of the car and drew his gun. "Halt!"

Will caught up with the girl and grabbed her arm. "What do you think you're doing, Viola?"

"Did you mean what you said in there? You really

don't love me?" Her southern drawl was laced with tears.

"I never told you I loved you. We went on maybe three dates. There never was anything between us."

Viola sobbed and dropped to the ground amidst the evening dew and cricket sounds.

Andy reached them and put handcuffs on the broken woman. "Viola Chastain, you are under arrest again. You have the right to remain silent …."

Once he finished reading her the Miranda rights, Andy guided her into the back of his squad car being careful to avoid hitting her head.

Katie watched from the porch.

Will waved to her. "It's all okay. We've got her."

Kate dropped into the swing as tears ran down her cheeks. She'd been the dumped one before. As much as she wanted to categorize her as a stalker, Kate knew in her heart that Viola was just another rejected girl.

After Andy pulled out of the yard with Viola, Will came and joined her on the swing.

"Ask me whatever you want to ask." He took her hand and squeezed it.

"I just don't want to be surprised like that again. I don't know your past since my mom got cancer." Kate looked up into his eyes.

"I dated Viola very briefly. Everything else she made up in her mind. I'm sorry she has caused so much pain. Why don't we go back in and eat?"

"There's still more to say about Viola Chastain." Kate nodded. "We can microwave the stew if you go get the microwave from the garage. We can talk later."

"This I can do, my dear." Will kissed her hand and helped her up from the swing.

They entered the dimming house and flipped on the lights. While Will went out to get the microwave, Kate gathered the bowls of stew and took them to the counter.

Perhaps the Bell Witch foolishness is over. Brian and Viola did a great job in concert to replicate the fearsomeness of the historic happenings; now that they are in the hands of the legal system, perhaps I can get on with my plans.

"Here's the microwave." Will came in with the device, slamming the back door closed with his foot. "Do you have other kitchen things to bring in?"

"Maybe one more box with cookie sheets, Bundt pans, and kitchen utensils."

"I could bring it in before we go home later." He set the oven on the counter and plugged it in.

She placed the bowls of stew in the microwave with paper towels over them and turned it on. As the time ticked down, she wrapped their muffins in a paper towel and added that for the final forty-five seconds. At the beep, she handed Will the muffins and his bowl of stew, then she joined him with her bowl.

They settled down to eat and talk about everything but Viola Chastain.

When dinner was over and two slices of cake had been consumed, Kate washed the dishes, and Will dried.

"You're going to want a dishwasher for your business." Will stacked the bowls in the cabinet where Kate indicated. "Between changing linens on the beds and in the bath, you'll not want to be washing dishes by hand every morning."

"I didn't even realize there wasn't a dishwasher until this afternoon." Kate unplugged the sink and scrubbed it as the water drained out. "I also want to get a check-in desk with slots for keys and room for a computer."

"You should have Clark at the antique shop look around for you." Will put away the rest of the dishes. "He could get you a good deal."

"I assume your mom will know where to go to find Clark?" Kate raised an eyebrow.

"Absolutely. I can go get that last kitchen box." Will leaned against the counter. "What else can we do here before heading back to Mom and Dad's?"

"It's already after nine. You have work in the morning. We should probably head back." Kate sighed. She was exhausted. She had stood most of the day punctuated with moments of sheer terror and hysteria. "I'm bushed."

"Tomorrow evening, we need to replace the hidden door to the cellar. Viola destroyed it in her rage to get in the passageway. I bet she cut that padlock off again. You need a better locking system. I'll check on it on my way to the garage."

Kate nodded. "I'll check upstairs to be sure any lights are off and finish up in here."

"Be right back with the box. I'll try to secure the cellar door too." Will headed out the back door.

The upstairs was dark. Kate turned off lights in the

living room and dining room, leaving the lights in the kitchen and at the front door on.

When Will came back in, he dropped the box on the floor and all the aluminum pans and utensils rattled. "Not much packing paper in here."

Kate shrugged. "It's not like they're going to break. I'm ready to go if you are."

"Before we go, I feel a need to clear the air." Will took her hand and led her to the red velvet living room settee. "You were upset with me when the evening began."

Kate wasn't sure what to say. "Yes, I was. You never told me anything about Viola or any other woman in your life. Guess I thought I was the only one. Totally unrealistic of me."

"You are the only woman in my life. At least the only one who matters, besides Mom, of course. My dating life consisted of a string of first dates. None of them ever measured up to you."

"You said you dated Viola three times." Kate's voice broke with a tremor of jealousy.

"The first was a blind date. The second was the first time we'd been alone. The third was when I told her there wouldn't be a fourth." Will put his arms around her, as best he could with her back brace. "You are special. You know how much. Are you jealous of a woman I called deranged this very evening?"

Kate sighed. "Of course not. I just … guess I was jealous given how much you mattered to her."

"It wasn't, isn't, mutual, Katie. You are the only girl who has ever mattered to me. I recognize how crazy that sounds. Those eight summers, we spent every waking moment together. Though it was very long ago, it mattered. I know who you are even if I don't know everything about you."

"I feel the same way, especially after Brian. Does he make you jealous too?" Kate leaned her head on his shoulder.

"Crazy jealous! I fought him in the parking lot of the hospital! I don't usually engage in brawling in public. The man is infuriating if nothing else."

Kate laughed. "Agreed. So, we're both linked with maniacs."

"Reminds me of that old Quaker saying. Goes something like, 'The whole world is crazy but me and thee, and sometimes I worry about thee.'"

"Okay, time to go back to your house and get sleep."

Will stood then helped her up. "What else could go wrong? We've solved the root cellar issues, the hidden passageway issues, and the secret saferoom in the attic issue."

"Oh, Will, don't ever say 'What else could go wrong?' There's always one more thing."

Chapter 26

One more thing …

"Rise and shine, sleepyhead." Maddy's voice heralded from Kate's door. "Shops open soon if you want to go antique shopping."

"What time is it?" Kate could tell that she'd overdone it yesterday when she rolled over.

"It's the-men-are-gone o'clock. Time for the women to have fun."

Kate laughed. "What time is 'the-men-are-gone o'clock'?"

"Eight-thirty. I made that coffeecake you like so well. The coffee isn't getting any hotter." Maddy had posted herself just inside the door leaning on the frame.

"Okay. I'll be down as soon as I take a quick shower." Kate roused herself and stood carefully. "I'm coming, Maddy."

"I'll get myself dressed and get my lists." Maddy left Kate to get herself together.

Kate and Maddy drove to the town strip in the bright August sun. It wasn't a big downtown. Along Hwy 41, they pulled into the driveway of a barn-like structure which had seen better days. An old rusty hay rake sat beside the parking area.

"I know it doesn't look like much, but trust me, Clark knows his business." Maddy climbed out of the car with her giant tote bag.

Kate exited her side of the car and followed Maddy into the "barn." Despite its outward appearance, the inside was a modern store with sliding doors that opened as they approached. The interior was enclosed and weather-proof. Marvelous old furniture lined the outside walls with many curiosities on shelves and tables down the center of the building. Old toys, kitchen doodads, workshop hand tools, estate jewelry, opera glasses and gloves, and things that defied Kate's knowledge.

"Good morning, ladies!" The man who approached them Kate assumed was the infamous Clark. He was an athletically built man dressed in jeans, tucked Oxford shirt, and a Mr. Rogers zipped sweater, even though it was August.

Kate shivered a bit. No wonder he wore a sweater; the air-conditioning was intense.

"I apologize for the indoor weather. Many of my best items would warp in the August heat and humidity. A/C is the best I have for climate control for my beautiful items, particularly the furniture." He shook Kate's good hand and gave Maddy an air kiss on each cheek with a hug. "It's been too long, Miss Maddy."

"Agreed, Clark. This is Kate Winslow …"

"Oh, the owner of Katharine's marvelous house on Spring Street! So very glad to meet you." His eyes grew large behind his round gold-rimmed glasses. "Let me know if I can take away any extra furniture you don't need. Your Aunt Kathy bought several nice pieces from me."

"I'll let you know, Mr. …"

"Oh, just Clark, darling. Last names are so superfluous." He waved away her formality. "But you are here for something special, correct?"

"Yes. I'm looking for a desk to put in the foyer from which to greet guests. You know, check them in, give them keys, use my computer."

"Hmmm. Let's see what I have. I assume you're looking for Victorian." Clark stroked his light beard. "Come with me."

He strode out across the store and down an outer aisle. He waved his hand over a mahogany desk. "Beautiful carving but utilitarian."

"It's a writing desk."

"Exactly. A Victorian writing desk. You don't want to clutter the foyer. You won't leave things piled up on it since it's the first thing your guests will see."

Kate struggled to keep her eyes from rolling. Maddy snickered behind her.

"I was thinking of something a little taller, with cubbies for room keys." Kate tried to be exact in her description though how to describe what she wanted eluded her while still being polite.

"Okay." Clark turned abruptly and walked around a bit. "Come see this." He led them to another desk. "Yes, another writing desk, but this one has cubbies. Still has the slim features with utilitarian usefulness."

"But I can't very well greet guests leaned over. It needs to be taller." *He doesn't listen very well, does he?*

"You don't plan to sit at this desk?" Clark's eyebrows bunched together. He assumed a thinking position, pursed lips, chin cupped in his palm with forefinger tapping his cheek. "Come look at this desk." He hurried to a back corner.

Compared to what he'd previously shown Kate and Maddy, this desk was hulking. A keyed fold down writing surface revealed cubbies and slots for various things. It had a stack of drawers on either side and a modesty panel in the knee area.

Kate sighed. *Perhaps I can plan to sit.*

"I know this is not what you're looking for. You want something like this but taller. Like a bank teller window. What you want is called a reception desk. I think I saw something like that on the web. Let me make some inquiries. Do you have a card?" Clark reached out for one.

Kate dug in her purse for one of her old cards. "The cell phone number is correct. Everything else is not."

"That's fine. You'll need new business cards for your B&B though. I'd be happy to have some at my checkout. In fact, most of Adams's businesses would welcome business from your guests. Spread them around town." Clark clucked and placed the card on his desk. "I'll call you when I find what you're looking for."

Maddy touched her shoulder. "Come on. We can browse on the way out."

Kate turned and followed Maddy. They oohed and aahed over various known and unknown items. Ultimately, she decided to save her money for the desk that wasn't a desk.

"Lunch?" Maddy held the door for her.

"I could eat." Kate joined her on a brief walk from

the antique shop to the diner.

As Kate finished her BLT, her phone buzzed. "Hmm. A text from Clark. 'Check out this piece I found online! Hurry back in so I can complete a deal for you before it sells.'" Kate clicked the link. "Look at this, Maddy."

Maddy took her phone and read the description out loud. "'A wonderful Victorian period hotel reception desk, bar or bank counter was hand carved of solid oak with green marble mounts about 1870 in England. Raised panels, the curved end and carved details are artistic. On the back is a kneehole with a floor, intended to work at stool height. Drawers have hand cut dovetail joints. The top cash drawer has a double throw working lock. There are dividers for ledgers and file books.' This reception desk is just what you're looking for, isn't it?"

Kate smiled. "Yes, it is. We should hurry down to Clark's shop and make a bid on it." Kate sent a text to Clark saying they'd be right there. She saved the picture of the desk on her phone and added it to her B&B Pinterest account, then she sent the picture to Will.

Maddy returned from the cashier. "Let's go buy a hotel reception desk!"

Kate and Maddy hurried along Hwy 41 back to Clark's barn. Clark was waiting for them at the door.

"I couldn't believe exactly what you wanted was available!" Clark hurried them back to the computer. "What do you think? Isn't it exactly what you are looking for?"

Kate sat in the chair Clark offered and gazed at the oversized computer screen. Solid oak with a curved end. Carved woodwork around it. Tall enough for a stool. Cubbies and file holders. A cash drawer as well. It was perfect. Hope filled her heart. *God, thank you for this encouragement. Maybe this will work. Maybe we are moving forward. I wish Will was here to be part of this.*

Just then, her text alert sounded. Will texted, "Yes! Perfect! Buy it!"

Kate handed her phone to Maddy.

"Yes! Billy says yes. You should get it." Maddy squeezed Kate's shoulders. "This is so exciting!"

Clark was fairly dancing around them. "Is that a yes? I love when the perfect piece finds the perfect owner. Let me get ahold of the seller. Browse while I make the call."

Kate browsed but strained to hear the phone conversation Clark was having with the seller of her new, old reception desk. It was her first real step of becoming a B&B owner. Butterflies fluttered in her stomach.

A new text from Will. *Hope you get it! It looks great. Wish I was there.*

Clark hung up and stood. Kate hurried toward him to hear the news.

"Congratulations! Your piece is being delivered next Wednesday. You just need to pay me."

Maddy hugged her. "This is so exciting!"

"Thank you both for your help." Kate gave her credit card to Clark.

While Clark ran her card, Kate called Will. When he answered, she quivered inside. "I got it. It's coming on Wednesday."

"Madame hotelier. It's official. You are running a

Bed and Breakfast in Adams, Tennessee."

His deep voice calmed her. Kate needed him to share her excitement as well as her trials. "I wish you were here too."

"Would you like to go out for dinner? You know, to celebrate."

Kate's stomach flipped. "Are you asking me out on a date?"

"I guess I am. If you want to call it that."

"Yes. I'd love to go on an official date with you tonight, you know, to celebrate." Kate couldn't control her smile.

"I should be there about six. Will you be at my house or yours?"

"Mine. I have some things to do there before then." Kate smiled. *A real date.*

"I'll see you then. I have a meeting to attend, so I have to go."

Kate hung up.

Clark returned with her credit card. "Congratulations. You're the proud owner of an antique reception desk."

"Thank you so much!" Kate squealed in her excitement. *And I have a date with Will Bell, no relation.*

193

Chapter 27

Becoming a Bed & Breakfast …

After Kate's big purchase, Maddy took her to her orthopedic doctor to remove her cast and evaluate her spine.

"Your x-rays show the arm has healed. We'll take the cast off today. You'll need to do some exercises to strengthen it." The doctor held another set of x-rays to the light. "Your back looks stable. Does it hurt you?"

"Only when I lie down at night and get up in the morning." Kate frowned. "What does that mean?"

"Time to stop wearing the back brace all the time. Wear it when you're home doing nothing. Gradually lengthen the time out of the brace. You need to allow your back to bend and flex. The vertebrae look cracked, but they seem unlikely to damage your spinal cord." He turned and looked at Kate. "You are one lucky lady. You should have died or ended up in a wheelchair. Don't take it for granted though. Another fall like that one will likely splinter your spinal column."

"I understand." Kate nodded. "It's not on my list of things to do again."

He turned to Maddy. "I know young adults are

hard to control. Whatever you can do to keep this lady out of harm's way would be a good thing."

"I'm not her mother." Maddy's face was turning deep pink. "I'm not sure I can affect anything she does."

"Then be a good friend to her." The doctor shook Maddy's hand, then he shook Kate's. "The nurse will be in to take off the cast. You can take off the back brace for a while today."

He was patient and attentive while in the examining room, but when he was finished, he whooshed out of the room with white coat flying to his next patient. The nurse came in, cut off the cast, and gave Kate instructions on strengthening her shriveled left arm.

When Kate and Maddy pulled up in front of the house on Spring Street, Joe was coming down a ladder on the front of the house. Victorian Seaside paint splattered the front of his coveralls.

"Joe! What are you doing?" Maddy put her hands on her hips. "Sally needs you. The baby's due any day."

He reached out and hugged Maddy. "Mom, I'm not the one who's pregnant. Sally's just fine. I have my phone on me at all times. We just live a couple blocks away."

Joe hugged Kate. "So, what do y'think? I took down the shutters. I'm not sure if we should replace them." He gestured to the pile of ragged wood shutters. "It looks more authentic without them."

"Thank you so much for your hard work. It looks great." Kate surveyed the front of the house. Now it looked more like the house Kate remembered.

"I still have more to do, but it's a start. I'll do what

I can this week." Joe wiped his hands with a paint rag. "Next week I'll need to start harvesting my field for sileage. The baby's due the end of August. Life gets more interesting then." He laughed.

"You and Sally come over for dinner. Katie and Billy are having their first date." Maddy winked at him.

"First date. That can't be right. Y'all are thick as thieves. Have been for nigh on twenty-five years." Joe put his hands on his hips. "Billy is definitely slipping and taking your good will and affections for granted."

"It's okay. We spend a lot of time together regardless." Kate felt that red wave creep up the back of her neck. "It's just dinner to celebrate my reception desk coming next Wednesday." She got out her phone and showed him the picture.

Joe whistled. "That's a beauty! Just like you."

Maddy punched him in the arm. "You are married. Don't flirt with Billy's girl."

"Ow, Mom! I'm just stating facts. Billy doesn't appreciate what's right in front of him. That's all I'm saying." Joe rubbed his arm. "I'm gonna go clean up, so I can go home to my wife. I'll be back in the morning, Katie."

Maddy carried the back brace as Kate climbed the front porch steps carefully. She'd been up and walking for most of the day. Pain radiated in her back.

"Wow! The guys have done great work in here. I can't get over how beautiful it is." Maddy laid the back brace on the couch. "Katie, you should probably lie down for an hour or so before Billy gets here."

"Agreed. Thank you for taking me shopping and to the doctor. Guess I can drive myself soon since I don't have the cast or brace." Kate hugged her. "You're a wonderful surrogate mom to me.”

“You’re too sweet, Katie-girl. You’ve been one of my crew since you were born. I’m just sorry to have missed the last fifteen years. That doesn’t mean you get a pass being part of us. See you back at the house after your dinner with Billy.”

“I probably can move back here tomorrow.” *I need to buck up and not be afraid to be here by myself.*

“You are welcome anytime, Katie.”

Maddy hugged her again, and Kate walked her to the door.

Kate waved until Maddy pulled away from the curb then locked the front door before going upstairs to lie down.

When Kate woke, the house was silent. She breathed a sigh of relief. The clock read five-fifteen. Will would be here at six. She took a quick shower then put on a summer skirt and tee shirt. She also pulled out a white sweater in case of cold air conditioning.

While Kate waited on Will, she went online to design Kate’s Bed & Breakfast business cards.

Will sat on the highway. He hadn’t moved even an inch in twenty minutes. *This is not the way I want to spend my life.* He rested his forehead on the steering wheel. *No wonder Brian didn’t want to drive back and forth from Adams. On top of that, I hate my job so far. All day at a desk in a cubicle, staring at a computer. What should I do?*

He moved forward about half a mile before

stopping again. *This is killing me bit by bit. I could be home with Katie. What can I do to work in Adams?*

He drove a few more miles then stopped. The clock read five-thirty. *I am not going to make it on time. I'm going to be late for our first real date.*

Oh, Lord, help Katie be okay with my lateness. The answer to his prayer came immediately. *Call her.*

He dialed her number and held his breath.

"Hi, Will. I'm not quite ready yet."

Will smiled to himself. Her voice cheered him more than he expected. "That's okay. I'm stuck on I-24. I'm not even to Joelton. When I get to the Hwy 431 exit, I'll get off there. I'd like to change before we head out. Is that okay with you?"

"You know it is. I'll be here whenever you can get here. Don't worry. I'll always be here for you."

"I thank God for you, Katie. I'll see you as soon as I can."

"No problem. I'll be ready whenever you show up."

When she hung up, Will came to a sudden realization. *My world revolves around Katie Winslow. I should have realized this before now. Without her, especially now, my world would collapse.*

Traffic started up at thirty miles an hour. *As long as it moves, I'm closer to Katie. I need to marry her. She's my One and my best friend.*

Chapter 28

Time to plan a business …

While she waited on Will to arrive, Kate plunged headfirst into planning the B&B. Her Music Business degree would come in handy in running her own business. Kate took her phone out front and took a picture of the house. Using the Canva website, Kate created a business card. She printed several pages of business card stock. Still no Will.

Kate began a trifold brochure, glancing at the clock as the time got later and later. She downloaded the house photo and the info from the business card into her project page. The sample she was using included three package deals. What could her B&B offer? First, she could offer a daily hot full breakfast, four freshly decorated Victorian bedrooms, and small-town charm and quiet. What did Adams offer? Antiques, Red River water activities, and the Bell Witch legend. Adams was very small, only 625 people were left behind by the building of I-24. Why would someone come to stay in small town Tennessee?

Some people on Facebook shared that they wanted to get away to read or to write without being interrupted. Kate did some research online. Some B&Bs offered packed lunches for picnics or hikes. Others included comfortable porch sitting and background music. Most offered all day coffee/hot tea stations. What about offering fresh baked cookies?

In addition to these services, how much per night or per package should she charge? She had so many important factors to consider to make her business successful.

When Kate looked at the clock, it was seven.

Will was an hour late. She called his phone. His ring tone could be heard on the front porch. She ran to the front door, flung it open, and threw her arms around his neck.

"I was so worried."

He hugged her and kissed her cheek. "I was becoming concerned myself. I haven't been home yet. Do you want to ride back to my house and visit with Mom while I change or go to dinner in these clothes?

They were face to face. His arms were around her and hers around his neck. She placed her lips on his and kissed him lightly. He took control of her lips and kissed them soundly. Then he released her.

"Guess we should have a first date before we get into kissing on your front porch in full view of the neighbors." Will gave a nervous laugh. "Dinner first or change first?"

Kate smiled. "You look fine. Depends on how you feel. Would you rather change into your jeans? Are you hungry?"

"Yes, and yes. Go grab your purse and keys. You can chat with Mom for a few minutes while I get more comfortable."

Kate hurried into the house. Along with her purse and keys, she picked up a couple of her new business cards to share with Will and his parents. At the last second, she grabbed her portfolio with notes about activity packages to offer at Kate's Bed & Breakfast.

While Will changed, Kate settled onto a bar stool with a cup of Maddy's coffee.

"Can I pick your brain, Maddy?"

Maddy laughed. "If you think there's anything of value up there, go for it."

"I'm working on a brochure to advertise the B&B. An example I'm using from Canva shows three activity packages being offered. I thought I could do something similar with Adams local attractions." Kate got her pen and opened the portfolio. "What do you think someone could do while visiting Adams?"

"Well, there's always the Bell Witch Cave and grounds, when it's open."

"I've got that. I'll have to talk to the guy that owns the grounds about that. He also has a Red River experience attraction. What else?"

"What about places to eat in town? It would bring income to people in Adams then."

"Maybe a meal ticket to places in town?" Kate nodded as she wrote it down. "What about a tour of the Bell Witch sites by the local historian? Would he be willing to do that?"

"I haven't met a person that he won't talk to." Maddy set out some baby carrots.

Kate took one. "I see on Facebook people who say they want to get away to read or write. How's the town's library?" Kate poised her pen, ready to write it all down.

"Adams doesn't have a library. Springfield has Stokes Brown Library. Clarksville has two in town and one on base. Cheatham County has one. Just about every county has one."

Kate puzzled over this situation for a moment. "What if I devised a scavenger hunt that took people to all the libraries in the area? And the historical society's museum at city hall? I could provide a prize each week to the most successful hunter. What if I offered event weekends, like those murder mystery dinners?"

"You've got some good ideas on your own. Let me know how I can help."

Kate handed her a business card. "What do you think?"

"It's beautiful!" Maddy put on her reading glasses. "It's very you. I love it."

When Maddy tried to hand it back, Kate refused. "Keep that. I made more. I'm going to need a source nearby for linens, towels, and Victorian specialty items for décor and welcome gifts."

"We could go tomorrow to a place I know while Will is in Nashville."

The word Nashville scraped across Kate's nerves. She couldn't lose Will to the big city. She wouldn't go back there unless she absolutely had no other choice. In addition to all that, Kate feared he'd have a life-altering accident in rush hour.

Maddy grabbed her hand. "You're shaking like a leaf. Something wrong, Katie?"

"I hate him driving to Nashville five days a week." She whispered so no one else in the house would hear. "I don't want to lose him to Nashville."

Strong arms wrapped around her from behind. Then Will whispered into her ear. "That's worry you shouldn't buy, Katie-girl. Nashville has nothing I need. I need you, though, in case you haven't realized that. I would gladly give up my job to have you in my life for always."

Kate closed her eyes. Tears leaked down her cheeks onto her sweater.

"Let's talk more at dinner. I'm starved." Will released her. "Don't worry, Mom. I know it's a school night. I'll be back early."

Maddy grinned. "Looks like some things are going very well."

Kate nodded and felt the heat rising in her face. She scooped up her promotional materials. "Yes, I think they are."

Will took her hand and led her down the driveway to his truck. Katie deserved better than his beat-up beast. He opened the door for her, and she slid in. Without the cast and the back brace, she seemed fragile. He came so close to losing her forever. She needed him. But more than that, he needed her.

"What's for dinner?" Her smile lit up the cab of the truck.

Even better, she made him smile. "I know an Italian place in Springfield."

"I don't need fancy." She touched his shoulder. "Just being with you is a treat."

Will couldn't help but smile. Katie just brought joy

inside him. She was right, of course. Anywhere with her would be great. "I think you'll like Angelo's. It's kind of a hole in the wall place."

"Sounds perfect."

Will pulled into a parking place in front of a small shop with the Angelo's Trattoria Pizzeria. He hurried around to open Katie's door and helped her out of the truck. As they walked to the door, the manager met them.

"Will, you know we close at 8. Can I make you a pie to go?"

Will sighed. He'd forgotten they closed early and that it was nearly 8 o'clock. "What do you want to do, Katie?"

"Let them fix us a pizza to go. We can eat in the town square we just passed."

Will ordered and paid for their special square Grandma pizza with cheeses and sausage then joined Katie on the picnic table out front. "I am so sorry. I knew they closed earlier than most places. They're local."

Katie reached across the table and took his hands in hers. "It really doesn't matter as long as we're together. Tell me about your new job. Make any friends? Learn anything new?"

He shook his head and laughed. "You make it sound like my first day in kindergarten."

Katie's sparkling laugh encircled him.

"I'm not enjoying my work. I sit at a desk all day, staring at a computer. I expected to be in the field more. The commute is painful. I'm wondering if I can find a way to set up my own business in Adams or Springfield or Clarksville." He squeezed her hand. "And I miss you when I'm so far away. I want to be available to find cool Victorian reception desks."

"Adulting can be hard." Katie gave him a spectacular smile. "I miss you when you're gone too. I began to picture you working with me at the B&B."

"What are these great ideas you have?" Will kissed her hand.

"Scavenger hunts, murder mystery weekends, Bell Witch legend weekends in October, activity packages." Katie's eyes lit up with excitement. "Writers' retreats, readers' retreats, board game retreats."

"Wow! You are revved up about these ideas. Sounds like a lot of fun. You'll need help if you're cooking and activity directing." *Could they do it together and survive financially?*

The manager stepped out of the pizzeria. "Here's your pizza, Will. Sorry I couldn't let you stay. We have things planned tonight."

"No worries, Max. I should have remembered that you close at 8."

"Introduce me to your friend." Max nodded toward Katie.

"Oh, this is Katie Winslow. She's renovating her great-aunt's Victorian to be a Bed & Breakfast. We've been friends since childhood. Katie, this is Max."

Katie walked over to shake Max's hand and handed him a business card.

"Do you mind if I call you sometime, you know, to go out?" Max wrapped his arm around her shoulders.

Katie shrugged out of his embrace. "I don't think that would be a good idea."

"No, she's my girl." Will's remark jumped out of his mouth unbidden. "I mean, we're dating."

"I thought you said she was your friend." Max narrowed his eyes at Will.

"It's complicated. We're still figuring it all out." Will stood and picked up the pizza. "Come on, Katie. Let's go eat this while it's hot. Thanks again, Max."

Will helped Katie into the truck and handed the pizza to her.

"Why don't we go back to the house and eat it?"

"What's wrong, Katie?"

"What are we? Friends, something more? We're technically on our first date. I can't believe you just shut him down before I could handle it." She wasn't smiling now. "Are you so unsure of me or of yourself?"

"I'd like to define that, but you asked me not to ask you the question I'm dying to ask." Will fingered the ring box in his pocket. *This isn't going the way I'd hoped.*

"Tonight's not the right night either. Why don't you just take me back to your parents' house? I'm not that hungry after all, and I'm feeling tired."

Will climbed in the truck and drove home with silence between them. The smell of pizza permeated the truck cab, but he had lost his appetite as well.

When they arrived at his home, Katie hurried up the stairs, leaving Will in the foyer with a large Grandma pizza.

"Smells good. You must have been to Angelo's." Dad took the box from him. "Come tell me what happened."

Chapter 29

Starting a new chapter …

Kate rose early and started gathering all of her things. She'd been here long enough that many of her possessions seemed to have taken up permanent residence. It was time they found a new home.

She really wasn't mad at Will. He told Max basically what she would have. He just assumed too much, and she was capable of handling herself. Was she Will's girl? Yes, if he wanted her, she was his … forever. *I should let him ask his question. Either way, I need to make Aunt Katharine's house my home.*

She heard him in the shower. *I can't let him leave thinking I'm mad at him.* Kate finished packing her suitcase. She'd need someone's help getting it down the stairs and to 415 Spring Street. Will's dad seemed able to help her most days. Kate looked around the guest room for any other items that belonged to her. That's when she spied an envelope under the door. *Oh, no!*

She rushed to pick up the note and opened it.

Dear Katie,

I'm sorry. You were right to call me on the carpet for my response to Max. It's not my business or place to determine who you date. It doesn't matter what I thought or felt. I hope to see you this evening if that's okay.

    Love, Will

Kate fanned the note back and forth as she considered her reply to Will's note.

The bathroom door opened, followed by the sound of Will's bedroom door opening and closing. A rap on her door startled her. On opening the door, Kate found Porter standing there.

He pointed to the suitcase on the floor. "I hear you're moving out today. Need help wrangling that luggage down the stairs?"

"Do you mind taking me to Aunt Katharine's house with it too?"

"No problem, Katie-girl. You know though that it's not Aunt Katharine's house. It's your house." He looked as though he had more to say but held his tongue. "After I have my coffee, we can go anytime."

"Thank you." Kate nodded. She had solved one problem today. Now if she could assuage Will.

Porter grabbed her suitcase and carried it down the stairs. Kate lingered to try to catch Will before he headed downstairs too.

Suddenly Will's door opened, and he stepped out in his dressier work clothes, khakis and a short sleeve dress shirt. Kate hurried to him, surprising him.

"Good morning, Katie. How are you feeling this morning?"

"Stupid. I messed up our first date."

Will took her hands. "No. That one's on me. I had no right to answer for you. I had no right to blurt out something I have no proof of. I can only say 'I'm sorry' and ask you to let me make it up to you."

Kate shook her head. "I shouldn't have taken offense."

Will pointed to the pile of linens in the floor in her room. "You're still leaving."

"It's time. I need to learn to live by myself in a creaky house with more mysteries than I know. I'll be fine."

He raised her hands to his lips and kissed them. "Can I see you tonight and bring pizza?"

"Of course. I love you."

He leaned in and gave her a soft kiss. "I'll stop by Angelo's for another Grandma pizza, then I'll come straight to your house."

"Sounds great. I have Coke in the fridge." She kissed him back.

"I better get going. I'll see you tonight." He leaned in for another kiss then hurried down the stairs.

Kate leaned against the wall and touched her lips. *Oh Kate. You have lost your heart to this sweet Tennessee farm boy/engineer.* She straightened up and bounced down the stairs for coffee.

When she reached the kitchen, Will was pouring his coffee into a to-go mug. Maddy was wrapping up a lunch for him. Porter was buttering a bagel.

"You're not going to eat breakfast?"

"No time, Sweetheart. I'll see you later." Will hurried to her and kissed her in front of his parents, then he whispered, "I love you too."

Once the front door slammed shut, Maddy raised her hands to the ceiling. "Praise God from whom all blessings flow! I've been praying for this day for years. Literally years! Welcome to the family officially."

"Now, Maddy, we don't know anything. Wait to praise God for the blessings once we hear the story. Get the girl some coffee. Katie, come sit down at the table."

Porter guided her to a seat, and Maddy produced a cup of coffee fixed to Kate's taste. She even brought over a croissant. Kate sipped her coffee and took her first bite.

Porter placed a hand on her wrist. "What happened? After last night I figured you were on the outs for a while."

Maddy sat down on the other side of her with her cup. "I knew you were moving out, but I was afraid you'd also banned Billy from the premises of your house."

"No, no, no. We were both tired. A stranger wanted to date me, and Will said no, I was his girl." Kate washed the flaky crust down with her coffee. "I was angry. Who was he to say who I could or could not date? After all, we weren't a defined couple."

Porter interrupted. "But you've spent near on every minute together since you moved into town. That's pretty exclusive."

"Porter, you don't know everything." Maddy harrumphed and went to refill her cup. "A girl doesn't like to be taken for granted. She wants to know what's going on. And she doesn't want to be told what to think. You'd think after thirty years of marriage you'd have figured that out." She slammed the pot just a little too hard and stirred just a bit too noisily. "What I want to know is what changed this morning?"

"I was feeling a little sad packing and didn't want Will to go to work without resolving our misunderstanding. He slipped a note under the door apologizing." She sipped her coffee. "I waited for him to come out of his room, and we talked."

"And kissed, I suwannee." Porter smacked the table with an open hand and all the dishes jumped.

Kate felt the red wave creeping up her neck into her face. She nodded. "We'll see what happens next, I guess." She caught a wink between Porter and Maddy. "What? Do you know something I don't? I know Will's carrying around a ring box in his pocket. I had told him not to ask me until I can say yes."

"Can you say yes now?" Porter rubbed his gnarled, scarred hands together.

Kate closed her eyes and thought for a second. "Yes, I believe I can."

Maddy whooped and knocked her cup of coffee over. Kate rushed for the roll of paper towels.

Will sat at his desk in a cubicle among many other nondescript cubicles. A man popped in and planted himself on the file cabinet. *Who was he? Bob, John, Tony?*

"Hey, Will. TGIF, dude. You've been here two whole weeks. How's it going?"

Anthony, his boss. "Okay, I guess. I've been watching training videos and filling out forms for two weeks. I'd like to do some actual engineering." *Because this computer is sucking the life from my soul.*

"I get ya. Mandatory stuff. I'll assign you to a project as soon as you complete the training and get through the binder of policies and practices." Anthony placed his hand on the three-inch D-ring binder on the end of Will's desk. "Can't have you making a big mistake on your first project, can we?"

My big mistake was thinking a desk job was my goal in life. "No, that would be unfortunate."

Anthony pounded him on the back and left the cubicle.

Will sighed and relaxed. Anthony returned.

"Hey, paychecks are direct deposited today. Like I said, TGIF!"

Will used the dreaded computer to access his pay stub. He was financially richer at least. *But is my soul worth a big paycheck?*

He loaded up another training video. *I hope Katie likes the big surprise I have for her. I can't wait to deliver it to her tonight*

.

Chapter 30

Popping up with a surprise …

The doorbell rang while Kate was cleaning the dust out of the library. Kate rushed down the spiral staircase then down to the first floor. When she opened the door, Andy was there in his uniform. *Not a social call then.* "Hi, Andy. What's going on?"

"Can I come in?" He shifted his weight onto his other foot.

"Of course, you can. Do you need a water, iced tea, or Coke?" Kate led Andy to the dining room table.

Andy sat next to Kate. "No, I'm fine. I'm here due to the restraining order you filed against Brian Montgomery. You said he had been gas-lighting you by using your phone through messenger. Is that correct?"

"Yes. I feel like an idiot about that." Kate felt the blush.

"Don't feel too bad about that. We arrested him for assault this morning. His DNA showed up on the crowbar that hurt Will. We'll be adding at least one other count to the assault charge to reflect the abuse you experienced from him." Andy pulled an official document out of the portfolio he carried. "I just need your signature agreeing that he participated in these abuses."

Kate read through the document, she signed the document. "So, it was Brian who left the bloody crowbar in my bed." She shuddered remembering that discovery. "Will he go to jail?"

"Hard to tell. I would think so due to the assault and the abuse charges." Andy put the document back in the portfolio. "Feel good that he's under arrest now."

After Andy left, Kate texted Will. *Brian has been arrested for assaulting you with that crowbar and for leaving it as a threat in my bed. They also plan to add abuse charges.*

Will wrote back, *Good to know he won't bother you anymore. I'll text you when I leave work.*

Will texted at four o'clock that he was leaving the office. Kate typed in a response. *Let me know when you're leaving Angelo's. I can't wait to see you!* Kate scanned the message to Will. *Does it seem too eager? Frightening? Desperate? Or did it convey her willingness to take their relationship to another level? Was that what she really wanted to say?* She hit send before she could change her mind. Her finger hovered over the undo choice until it disappeared.

The response was heartening. *I called ahead. Pizza ordered and in the oven. Supposed to be ready by 4:30. I've also got a surprise for you!* The text ended with a heart emoji.

A surprise? Should I tell him 'yes' tonight? Kate sent him back the same heart emoji. After putting her phone aside, she laid a tablecloth and set the table with her grandmother's china and stemware. A little formal for pizza, but she had a feeling it was a special meal. She put a large trivet on the center for the pizza, so it wouldn't get grease on the cloth. She'd picked up sparkling grape juice to serve and whipped up a chess pie for dessert. Everything was ready.

At 4:30, Will texted that he was leaving Angelo's. Fifteen minutes later, she heard a knock at the door. Kate opened the door to Will, holding out the pizza box.

"Peace offering." He winked. "I have the surprise in the truck. Set this on the table and come back to the door." Will dashed down the porch steps and ran across the yard.

Kate took the pizza in, wondering what he was up to. She returned to the porch to see Will carrying a white wicker basket across the lawn. He hid the contents of the basket with a blue plaid blanket over it.

"What are you up to? Is this your laundry? Did your mom get tired of doing it for you?"

He laughed. "No, nothing like that." He set the basket on the porch and pulled back the blanket. "This darling is Beebe."

A white lab puppy, like on all the commercials, spilled from the basket onto the porch.

"Oh, Will, he's beautiful." A sparkle from beneath Beebe's chin caught Kate's eye. "What's this?"

She pulled the puppy into her lap. Beebe was a cuddly, fuzzy, warm armful. Kate read a note hanging from the large blue bow tied on his collar. "Will you marry us?" The engagement ring she'd feared dangled from the blue ribbon.

"Yes, Will. I'll marry you. I'm also keeping the

dog."

Will kneeled beside her on one knee. He took her chin in his hand and kissed her. As they kissed, Beebe wriggled loose and ran to the porch steps. Before they could stand to catch him, he was in the front yard, heading for the street.

"Stay here. I'll get him." Will launched himself off the porch and chased the dog into the street. A car came to a screeching stop just as Will grabbed Beebe.

Kate closed her eyes, not wanting to see Will or Beebe splattered across the road.

"You can open your eyes. We both survived. And Terrance says 'hi.'" Will laughed and handed the dog to her.

She snuggled her face into his fur.

"Pizza is getting cold. Let's put Beebe in the back yard, without the engagement ring." Will took Beebe, untied the blue bow, rescued the ring, and then released the puppy into the fenced backyard.

Kate poured the juice and served each of them a piece of pizza while he was in the yard. When she turned to see what was keeping him, she found him on one knee, offering her a sparkly diamond ring.

"Will you marry me, Kate Winslow?"

She knelt beside him. "Yes, Will Bell. I'll marry you, my best friend."

They embraced, then Will helped Kate up from the floor.

Once they sat at the table, they called Maddy.

"Hello? Everything okay, Billy?"

"Yes, they are. We're calling to tell you …," Will began.

Kate finished, "We're engaged!"

Maddy's shrieks could be heard all over Robertson County. "Porter, get in here!"

"What's going on, son? Why is your mom whooping and hollering?"

"Katie and I are engaged, Dad." Will shrugged.

Kate laughed. "We're getting married."

"Well, hot dog!" Porter dropped the phone and left Kate and Will hanging.

Will hung up. "Guess they're happy about our news."

"Of course, they are." Kate kissed him.

A bark at the back door caused her heart to jump. She hurried to let Beebe in.

Sunday morning, Kate was finally going to church with Will. Between the hospital and basic destruction, she had missed services all summer so far. And she got to drive her car for the first time since she'd arrived in Adams. Now if she could get there on time.

She looked in the bathroom mirror to check her make-up. She needed to make a good impression.

Beebe ran around her ankles.

"Darling, you are going to trip me, then everyone will say I don't need a dog. Get in your crate."

Beebe's tail nearly wagged off as he ran to the crate that sat in the corner near Kate's bed. He plopped in it and panted for approval.

"Good dog." Kate brought him a treat and closed the gate. "I'll be home soon. You can snooze while I'm gone. I'll always come back."

He yipped and gave her a doggy smile.

Kate slipped on some dress shoes and picked up her purse. *I hope I'm wearing the right clothes for the small-town worship services at Red River Baptist.* The church had been founded in 1791. According to the books she'd read, the church had thrown John Bell out for not attending regularly prior to the "hauntings" of the Bell witch. To say it was historic was an understatement.

She slipped into her car and opened the garage door with the new automatic opener Will had installed for her. *Such a sweet man!* As she gripped the steering wheel, the diamond on her left hand sparkled. *I get to literally marry my best friend!* Kate grinned at the thought and backed her car out into the alley. *No Bell Witch on the garage doors, praise God.*

People were gathering in the parking lot of the church as Kate pulled in. Will stood next to his truck in a space he was saving for her. She slid her car into the spot. When she turned off the engine, Will opened the door for her.

He gave her a grin. "I'm so glad to see you this morning. I missed having breakfast with you at Mom and Dad's." He bent and kissed her. "Did you and Beebe sleep well last night?"

"We did. No weird sounds or disturbances."

"Hopefully that is over."

Kate snuggled into his embrace as they climbed the steps to the entrance of the church. "I was beginning to believe the Bell Witch was real."

"Don't say those words out loud, especially here at the Bell family church." Will looked solemn but then burst into laughter. "Kidding."

A young woman approached them. "I hear congratulations are in order, Billy."

"Thanks, Sarah. This is Katie Winslow, my fiancée."

"You're the one fixing up the house on Spring Street." Sarah offered her hand. "I run the bakery in Springfield. If you decide you need something, I'd be willing to go into business with you."

Kate shook her hand. "That sounds great. Maybe you could provide snacks for packed lunches or teas. Maybe I can offer birthday parties too."

"If you can get people to want to come here, I'm sure you'll do well."

"Sarah, come on! The organ music has started." A young man called to her from the front doors.

"My husband, Paul. I'd like to come by and see what you're doing to the old house."

"I'd like that. Come by most any time." Kate and Sarah hugged briefly.

Will and Kate followed her up the steps and into the hush of the sanctuary. After the bright sunshine, the room seemed dark. Will led Kate to the "family pew" and guided her in next to Joe and his very pregnant wife, Sally.

As the service ended, Sally stood to hug Kate. "Welcome to the family, Katie. If I can help you navigate the family dynamics, let me know. Oh, my!"

The whoosh of amniotic fluid took them both by surprise.

"Joe! It's time."

Joe picked her up and carried her to their car and headed out to the hospital. Maddy and Porter weren't far behind.

Will walked with Kate down the steps to the parking lot. "Why don't you drive your car home, and I'll pick you up there?"

Kate nodded and jumped in her car.

When she arrived home, she parked in the garage and closed the carriage doors using the new closure system. *Will is so capable with his workman's hands.* Kate gathered her things and turned to open the car door and startled at what she saw.

Terrance stood beside the car and opened the door for her. "Good morning, Kate. Can I help you with your things?"

"You gave me a fright! What are you doing in my garage?"

"Oh, I just slipped in to surprise you. I'm glad you're able to drive now." Terrance took her Bible from her hands. "Just hadn't seen much of you lately. I thought I'd drop in and say hello."

"I'm afraid I'm not here for long. Will and I are headed to the hospital. Sally, Joe's wife, is in labor at Northcrest Hospital."

Terrance walked with her to the kitchen door. He took her left hand and touched the engagement ring on her finger. "I see you have a sparkler on your left hand. Will?"

Kate took her hand back. "Yes, Will asked me recently." A basic sense of unease crept into her body. An involuntary shudder shook her.

"Hospitals are often cold. You should take a sweater." He handed her Bible back to her. "I just wanted to see you. We never did get to do our movie binge night. Guess it will never be arranged now that you plan to marry Will."

"Why not? We're still friends, right?" Kate shuddered again, but it wasn't cold that caused it since it was August in middle Tennessee.

"Great! Say when and I'll adjust my schedule." At her nod, he continued. "I'll let you go on and get a sweater. Give Joe and Sally my congratulations."

Will opened the kitchen door. "There you are. I've been waiting out front for you."

Terrance glowered at him. "She was just talking to me."

"No problem, I just wondered where she had been distracted."

Kate hurried up the steps to the kitchen. "I need to grab a sweater. Good to see you, Terrance." She ran up the staircase to her bedroom. When she got there, she collapsed on the bed and shook. *What is it with Terrance today?*

223

Chapter 31

A new Bell is born ...

Will and Katie pulled up in front of Northcrest Hospital in Springfield. Will opened the door for Katie. *I am the luckiest man in the world!*

"Aren't you excited about a baby in the family? You'll be Uncle Billy." Katie took his arm.

Will shook his head. "I'm never going to lose that name, am I? Remember you're signed up to be Auntie Katie."

"And lucky to be yours and Aunt Katie to Joe and Sally's child." Katie squeezed Will's arm. "Did Terrance seem a little off today?"

"Terrance's moody and passionate. Makes him a great firefighter."

When they entered the hospital foyer, Dad ran to them. "Where have you been? The baby's coming any minute." He grabbed Will's other arm and dragged him to the elevator with Will pulling Katie along as well.

They got off on the maternity ward floor where Maddy was waiting. Porter hurried to her and took her in his arms.

"We could be here ourselves next year." Will

whispered into Katie's ear.

"Not if we're not married in the next three months."

"Guess we need to set a wedding date, huh?" Will hadn't even thought about when they'd get married. *What's wrong with me anyway? Katie makes me addled.*

A nurse appeared at the door to delivery. "Mr. and Mrs. Bell?"

Mom and Dad stood. "Yes?"

"Congratulations, Grandma and Grandpa. It's a lovely baby girl."

After making a sufficient fuss about the little one named Mandy, Will and Katie headed back to Katie's house. Will made sure space was clear for the reception desk that was arriving on Wednesday.

When late afternoon came, Will and Katie took a Coke break on the porch swing, then he drove into Springfield to bring back burgers and fries.

When dusk arrived, they returned to the porch swing. Katie pointed out the fireflies that Will would have overlooked. As it grew dark, they tussled with Beebe until Will needed to go home to be able to go to work on Monday morning.

Kate woke in the middle of the night to the sound of Beebe moaning and crying.

"What's wrong, little one? Everything's okay."

Beebe continued whimpering. Kate slid out of bed and sat down outside the crate.

"You can't sleep in my bed, sweet Beebe. You've not had this problem before. What's going on?"

He moaned and scratched at the crate.

"Do you need to go out?" Kate unlatched the gate, and Beebe catapulted into her arms. "Poor darling. Is your tummy upset?"

That's when she heard it. Movement inside the walls.

Kate carried the puppy down to the back yard and let him loose. With her cellphone flashlight, she went to check the root cellar doors. Beebe came with her and sniffed and whined. The padlock had been cut again, and the doors lay open.

"Not again!" Kate called the Robertson County Sheriffs number in her phone. When they answered, she said, "Someone is in my house again."

She tied her robe together and scooped up the puppy. She walked around front and sat on the porch steps to wait for the sheriffs.

Andy pulled up first. He jumped from the car and ran to the porch. "Are you okay?"

"I'm annoyed as much as anything. Beebe woke me up. I guess he heard whoever it is first. The lock is cut on the root cellar doors again."

A second car rolled up to the house. The officer strode up the walk to the porch. "Sgt. Frank Algood." He nodded. "This is an intruder alert, correct?"

Kate nodded. "Yes, the house has an extensive hidden passage system. The root cellar is not as secure as it should be, and people can access the passageways and the house from there."

Just then, a window broke, and smoke poured from it.

"No, no, no!" Kate held the dog closer. "Terrance is just a couple doors away, isn't he?"

Sgt. Algood was already calling the fire department.

Within minutes, Terrance was on the front lawn with a long garden hose in his turnout gear. Fire truck sirens began, and the Adams Volunteer Fire truck pulled up into the yard. Firefighters poured from the truck as the fire breached the roof.

Kate called Will. "I hate to disturb your sleep, but I thought you'd like to know that someone broke into the house and set it ablaze. The firefighters are here as are Andy and Sgt. Algood. There's probably nothing to be done. I just needed to tell you."

"I'll be right there."

Soon water was pouring into the attic, no doubt ruining all Aunt Katharine's memories and the antique wedding dress that Kate had hoped to wear. She sat down on the curb with Beebe and cried.

Will parked near her, jumped from the truck, and made his way to her. He sat down beside her and wrapped his arms around her.

"Beebe probably saved my life." Kate sniffled.

Will handed her the pocket handkerchief from his jeans back pocket. "Then it's a good thing I got him for you." Beebe wriggled over to Will's lap. "Were you able to save anything?"

"What you see is all I have." Kate looked up at the blaze. "My purse is in there!"

"Go sit in the truck with the dog. I'll see what I can find out."

Will walked around the hoses and paraphernalia in the yard and found Terrance in the backyard near the root cellar doors.

"Terrance, what happened here?"

"Can't tell you a lot right now. The damage is primarily in the attic and roof. The rest of the house will have some smoke and water damage."

"Katie's purse is in her room on the second floor. Can someone locate it and bring it out for her?" Will coughed after inhaling some smoke.

"I'll send someone after we're sure the flames are out."

Will nodded. "Thanks. Should I take her back to my parents' house?"

"Yes, the inspector will be here in the morning. She might as well get some rest in the meantime."

"You know how to get ahold of us, I presume."

Terrance shook Will's hand. "I'll give her a call when I know something."

When Will returned to the truck, Andy was interviewing Katie. "When did you wake up?"

"It was around two when Beebe started crying."

"Did you hear anything besides the dog?"

"Not at first. I heard movement in the walls after Beebe woke me up. When we went out into the backyard, I found the root cellar doors open and the padlock on the grass."

"Suspicions concerning who it could be that broke in and set the fire?"

Katie nodded. "The same two that have been in my business already: Brian Montgomery and Viola Chastain. Beyond that, I don't know."

Will got in the truck. "We're headed to my house. Terrance will look for your purse and contact us in the morning. The fire inspector will be out then too."

He started the truck and drove back to his house with Katie.

Mom and Dad were in the kitchen with a fresh pot of coffee when they arrived. Beebe scampered through the house and found Will's dog Walker. Katie sank onto a bar stool at the counter.

"I just can't do this."

"What do you mean, Katie-girl?" Mom went to her and hugged her. "You can do anything you set your mind on."

"You didn't see it, Maddy! Flames were shooting out through the roof. My reception desk is coming Wednesday. The house is not fit to open now. I'll have to file insurance and hire a contractor to repair the roof and all the other damage that's been done to it. At the end of the day, someone could vandalize it again." Katie sipped her coffee. "I can't keep using your home as an Air B&B."

"No one has a problem with you being here. Leastwise none of the occupants." Porter offered a refill on coffee. "Maybe you might think on giving up on the house. We've got plenty of room here, especially after you marry."

Will stood behind her and wrapped her in his arms. The diamond on her left hand sparkled in the kitchen light. "I saw it. Katie, you can do whatever you set your mind to. I'm in, no matter what happens. Let's see what the sheriffs discover and what the insurance company will do. You don't have to decide tonight. Go on to bed. I'll stay home tomorrow and help you."

Will escorted her upstairs. When they reached the guest room, he wrapped his arms around her. "My love, as long as we have each other, we can do anything."

"I know, but I'm worn down. I've been hurt, you've been hurt, the house has been hurt."

He squeezed her tight. "God's got this. Go to sleep. Beebe is waiting on you."

Katie opened the door, and the wriggly puppy came squirting out into her arms. Beebe licked her face and rubbed up against her. "Okay, you can sleep with me tonight."

"Lucky puppy." Will kissed Katie. "The best reason to get married is to not have to say good night."

"This is your parents' home. Behave. Good night, sweetheart." Katie slipped into the guest room with Beebe.

Will put his hand on her door. *God, Keep her safe.*

SURVIVING RENOVATION

Chapter 32

Fixing the house …

Kate waited for the insurance agent on the front porch while Will explored the house. The first and second floors had minimal damage, but the attic were nearly destroyed. Fortunately, the turret with the library was preserved intact. Great-Aunt Katharine and Great Grandma Katerina had many first editions in their library; It was part of her readers weekend plan.

Will and Andy were poking around in the root cellar, looking for clues of the intruder and arsonist. Kate felt she knew who would want to destroy her dream: Brian Montgomery. What a horrible thing for him to do while declaring his love to her. Besides that, he would have violated the restraining order to have been in the house with her.

The car with an insurance logo on the door pulled up out front, so Kate hopped up to greet him.

"Kate Winslow, I presume." He shook her hand. "Mark Argent. What a beautiful house!"

"Except for the burnt parts."

"We can fix all that. Do you have the fire inspector's report?"

"Not yet. He's coming by today sometime. I guarantee it was arson. I wasn't alone in the house. I heard movement, then I went outside with my puppy. The next thing I knew, the house had smoke billowing from the roof."

"Sounds like arson." Mark took out a notepad and started writing information. "Can we go inside?"

"Of course. My fiancé and an officer from the Sheriff's Department are inside." Kate opened the front door to him. "Should I walk with you?"

"Absolutely. I want to hear your dream for this house. I want to help you achieve your plans."

Kate smiled. "I love that."

She showed him around the downstairs, which looked fine except for the smoke in the air and streams of water running down the new wallpaper. She showed Mark the hidden passage, which seemed okay.

The staircase to the second floor was in good shape, and her bedroom was safe.

Will met her in the hallway. "Can I borrow you?"

"Sure. Mark, this is my fiancé, Will Bell. Feel free to roam as you need to."

"No problem, Kate. I'll catch up with you before I leave."

She left Mark to join Will. "What's up?" She took Will's hand.

"Come look at this." He led her up to the attic.

On the floor was burned a message, "If I can't have you, no one else can."

"Brian. Did Andy see this?"

"Yes, but he pointed out that Viola could have written it too."

Kate shook, with fear, anger, and lack of sleep.

Who would do such a thing? Brian had never been violent before Will. I never would have considered marrying him if he had been.

Will wrapped her in a hug. "It's going to be okay. I won't let anyone hurt you."

She nodded. "I know, but you can't control …"

"Only God is always everywhere. Whatever I can control, I will."

A knock on the front door caused them both to race downstairs with giggles and running into each other. Will got there first and flung open the door.

A short man with a clipboard stood there. "Good morning. I'm Glen Hadron from bed and breakfast inspections."

Kate arrived winded. "Kate Winslow. Did you say bed and breakfast inspections? Today's an awful day to inspect. We had a fire last night, probably arson."

"Is the kitchen affected? I can take a look at the grounds, then when you've repaired the fire damage, I can work with that part."

"Will Bell, fiancé. How can I help?" He shook the inspector's hand.

Glen looked at the porch and up at the ceiling. "I will start on the outside, then work my way in. Will you be living in the property?"

"Yes, with a white Labrador." Kate looked at Will and grimaced.

"On-site. Pet. Got it. I'll just poke around and make notes for you." Glen disappeared around the corner of the wrap around porch.

"Of all the days for him to show up." Will took Kate's hand and smiled. "It will all work out."

Before she could close the front door, a moving

van pulled up in front of the house.

"What? The reception desk isn't supposed to be here until tomorrow." Kate covered her eyes and leaned against the door jamb.

Two burly men left the van and headed up the walk; one was waving paperwork. They lumbered up onto the porch.

"You Kate Winslow?" The one with the paperwork handed it to her. "We got a funky looking desk to deliver."

Will stepped in and shook hands with each of them. "Great. It goes right here in the foyer." Will followed the men out to the truck.

Kate went out on the porch with Beebe and sat in the swing. It was just too much to handle. Too much to cope. Perhaps she should just give it up.

"Hey, what's being delivered?"

Kate startled and turned to find Terrance coming from beside the house. Beebe whined and growled a little in the back of his throat.

"Hi, Terrance. How did you come from the back?"

"Garage was open." He took the porch steps two at a time. "How are you doing after the fire?"

Why was the garage open? If it wasn't open, how and why would Terrance get into the backyard? Will's truck was parked on the street in front of the house. He wouldn't have opened it.

As Terrance came closer, Beebe barked and growled at him.

"Stop, Beebe. Terrance's a friend." Kate pulled on his leash to get him closer to her and away from Terrance's entrance.

"I usually get along fine with dogs." He held his

hand out.

Beebe snapped at it and bared his teeth.

Terrance snatched his hand back. "Guess I'm a stranger danger to him."

Kate pulled Beebe into her lap. "What is wrong with you?" *Is he trying to warn me about Terrance? Why?* She pulled Beebe closer.

Terrance chuckled. "Guess you can't fool all of them all of the time." He sat on the top porch step. "What's going on today?"

"Too much. Insurance agent, fire inspector, state bed & breakfast inspector. And as if that wasn't enough, the antique desk I ordered came a day early after the fire last night." Kate leaned her head back and sighed. Beebe climbed up to her face and gave her puppy kisses. She laughed at the dog.

"Why don't we take a walk? Put the dog in the backyard. You need to get away, at least for a few minutes."

"You win. A short walk would do me good." Kate picked up the puppy and put him in the backyard. She made sure to latch the gate. "Okay, let's go see what's happening in Adams today."

Will helped the delivery guys place the desk. It was a beauty. Just like it had time-traveled from Victorian days straight to Katie's foyer. He stepped out onto the porch where he'd seen her last with the dog. No Katie. No Beebe. *Hmm.*

He stepped back into the house and abruptly met

up with Glen Hadron, the state inspector.

"Mr. Bell, here is Ms. Winslow's rating. It must be displayed in a prominent place." He ripped a page from the pad. "I can come back to give you a passing score once the fire-damaged areas have been repaired. You will need a sanitizing dishwasher as well. Questions?"

Will shook his head. "Can she call you later with any questions?" *Katie should be here to ask them.* He called her phone and heard it ring in the kitchen. "Hold on, Mr. Hadron."

Will chased the ring to Katie's purse on the table. *Where is Katie?* She wouldn't leave her purse behind. A yip at the back door indicated that Beebe was not on a neighborhood walk with her. He returned to the foyer and Mr. Hadron.

"I'm not sure where Katie is at the moment."

"Here's my card. She can call me if she needs more information."

Will saw him out and returned to the back door to let Beebe in. "Where is your mama? She shouldn't be too hard to find in that hot pink tank top she's wearing." He took Beebe up to his crate and started searching for Katie.

Chapter 33

Playing with fire …

Kate and Terrance walked around the block ending at Terrance's house just two doors from hers.

"Come in for a Coke?" Terrance grasped her elbow. "You should see how my house looks in comparison to yours."

Kate's 'something isn't right meter' was sending out frantic warnings. "I really should get back. I left Will handling the arson investigation, the insurance guy, and the state inspector. Oh, and the arrival of my reception desk. He's probably looking for me by now."

She tried to take back her elbow from his grasp, but his fingers held firm.

"I insist, Kate. You must come in." His eyes narrowed. He guided her up the walkway and onto the porch.

The paint on the porch was old and peeling. The swing looked ready to collapse in on itself.

Terrance opened the front door and pulled her inside. His Victorian house needed serious repair. The wallpaper was peeling. The floors were scuffed and dull. The carpet on the stairs was worn.

"You can fix most of this." She pulled at her elbow, and he held on tighter. "You're hurting me, Terrance."

"Of course, if I had friends coming out of the woodwork, quite literally in your case, I could accomplish a renovation like yours. Unfortunately, I just don't have the money or connections to make that happen." He turned her towards the steps and pulled her up to the second floor. He shoved her into a bedroom onto a squeaky brass bed.

"What are you going to do?" Her voice rose to a high pitched strangle on the last word. "I thought we were friends."

"Take off that engagement ring, and we still can be friends." He lifted her left hand and fiddled with the diamond in Will's ring.

"Why? I agreed to marry him." She wasn't sure what to say. Terrance had turned into a jealous monster. The man before her was not the brave hero she imagined him to be.

"I want the ring and the promise gone. I could redo the whole first floor with the cash from that ring alone." Terrance grabbed the ring and tried to force it from her finger. "Besides, you are supposed to marry me. I knew it from the moment we met. If not me, then no one else can have you."

Kate's left arm, even without a cast, couldn't withstand Terrance's strength. He finally wrenched the ring off her hand. Her stomach flipped as she recalled the words burned into the wood floor: "If I can't have you, no one else can." *He's the arsonist. Was it Terrance who hit Will with the crowbar? He was in the house when I fell into the safe room.* She breathed a prayer for rescue from this mad man.

Terrance pocketed the diamond ring. "Well, you made your choice. You are making me do this to you. Why wasn't I good enough?"

Kate had no words. "What are you going to do to me?"

"Only what I'm good at, dear Katie. Remember, you had a choice." Terrance left the room and slammed the door shut.

Kate heard a latch slide into place on the outside of the door. "Terrance! Don't do this!"

A wicked laugh responded to her cry.

Kate ran to the windows and attempted to open them. The old casements were swollen and had been painted closed. The stubborn sash wouldn't budge. Her weak left arm couldn't break it loose. She banged on the glass as tears streamed down her face.

Will, come and get me. Find me before it's too late. Kate sagged against the window and wept. *Lord, help me in my hour of distress. I know I haven't given You first place in my life. Forgive me. Rescue me as only You can.*

She felt more than heard the whoosh of fire taking root in the hallway outside the latched door.

Will searched for Katie in her house, including the secret passages and attic. In the fire-ravaged attic, he found a wedding dress draped across a rocking chair. Both showed signs of smoke and water damage. Had she planned to wear it on their wedding day?

He left the house through the kitchen and headed for the garage. Her car was still there, but the doors to the alley were open. He looked up and down the alley. She might have been feeding that stray black cat from her first day here. No Katie was there to be seen. *Where could she be?*

Suddenly, Will felt a nudge in his spirit. *Find me. Save me. Will, come get me.* He shook his head. The messages from nowhere resounded inside him. *Katie's in danger!*

That's when he smelled the smoke and heard window glass popping.

He closed the doors to the alley and locked the door to the garden. He ran around the house to the street. Smoke was coming from Terrance's old Victorian house.

A new message entered his head. *I love you, no matter what may come of this. Know you were loved.*

Will rushed down the street to Terrance's house. Fire had breached the roof, and smoke billowed from broken windows. *Where are you, Katie?*

The volunteer fire squad arrived, pulling their truck up into the front yard. Will watched for Terrance, but he wasn't with them. *Was he in the house as well?*

Chaos reigned around him as the firefighters claimed the scene. The cacophony shrank around him as he looked up at the house. In the front windows on the second floor, something bright pink caught his eye. Her bright pink tee shirt! "Katie!" She was slumped against the window.

As a firefighter passed him, Will grabbed his arm and pointed to the window with the pink shirt. "That's my fiancée. We have to save her!" Will realized then there was decorative ironwork barricading the windows. She couldn't escape through the window without taking the grating off.

"Stay back, Billy. There's a ladder truck on the way from Springfield. We've got giant bolt cutters that will work on the grating. Just hang tight."

"How long can she stay in that window? How long before smoke inhalation overwhelms her?" Will struggled with the firefighter to get to the house, but then he heard a low siren ending as the ladder truck pulled into the yard.

"Not a moment longer than it will take." He hurried off to talk to the ladder truck crew.

Will saw the man gesture to the window where Katie was trapped. The crew nodded and started raising the ladder and extending it to the window.

243

Chapter 34

Yet another ambulance ride …

A firefighter climbed the ladder with an enormous pair of bolt cutters. When he reached the window, he tapped the bolt cutters on the glass on the corner away from Katie. Old rainbow glass showered down like flickering diamonds, allowing smoke to escape and fresh air to reach Katie. Then he began cutting away the decorative ironwork.

"Coming down!" The ironwork fell into the bushes in front of the porch.

The man with the bolt cutters used them to break the glass more until they reached where Katie leaned against it. A second man climbed the ladder and stepped through the window where the glass had been. He lifted her in his arms while the first man broke out the remaining glass. Finally, they worked together to get Katie down the ladder and handed her off to the waiting EMTs.

Will rushed to Katie's side at the ambulance. They were pumping air into her lungs to help her expel the toxic smoke-filled air she had inhaled. Her pale and limp body frightened him. He took her hand and squeezed it. That's when he noticed. She wasn't wearing her engagement ring. What happened to her? Where is Terrance?

Another gurney appeared from behind the house holding a closed body bag.

"Who is it?" Will walked over to the stretcher.

"You're not going to be able to identify him. Looks like the start of the fire was self-immolation by this man. He was outside the room your girl was in. The door was locked and bolted. He didn't intend on surviving, nor did he intend on Katie escaping." The firefighter wheeled the stretcher to the coroner's van.

It had to be Terrance. Who else could it be?

"Hey, Will!" John, one of the Adams Volunteer Firefighters, jogged up to him. "Found something your Katie may be missing." He reached in his pocket and pulled out Katie's misshapen engagement ring. "Is this what I think it is?"

Will nodded. "I hope she survives to wear it again. Thanks, John, for spotting it."

Katie's cough drew Will's attention, and he ran to the gurney.

When he got to her side, she wrapped both arms around him. He pulled her close.

He whispered, "I thought I'd lost you."

She continued to cough but nodded that she agreed.

"Terrance is dead."

"Sorry to break up this reunion, but we need to get your girl to the hospital to determine how bad the smoke inhalation is. Climb in."

After the EMTs lifted the gurney into the ambulance, Will took a seat beside her.

Will clasped his hands around one of hers and closed his eyes. *Lord, I'm so grateful to be in the ambulance with the living victim and not the one headed to the morgue. Bring my Katie back to me. We've made this trip too many times this summer. Protect her from further harm. In Your name, Amen.*

When he looked down at Katie's face, her eyes were fixed on him. The oxygen mask made it hard to be understood, and every word was punctuated by a smoke-induced coughing fit.

"Don't try to talk, Miss Winslow. It just exacerbates the smoke inhalation." The EMT squeezed her other hand, then adjusted the oxygen flow.

Will gave her the best smile he could muster. "It's okay. I'm not going anywhere without you."

Katie pulled her naked left hand from the EMT. She pointed to the ring finger.

"I have it." He pulled it from his pocket. "It needs a little repair." Even though the gold band had become misshapen in the fire, the diamond sparkled under the lights in the ambulance.

She nodded. "What happened… to… Terrance?" The coughs punctuated her words.

"Dead. He set himself on fire."

Katie shook her head and tears streamed down her cheeks.

Will kissed her right hand. "Nothing you could have done, Katie. He was determined. Not only did he set the fire at your house, apparently he was under suspicion for several others in the area. That represents a lot of pain inside Terrance."

Tears ran down her face.

The ambulance bumped into the hospital parking lot and swung around to the Emergency Department entrance.

Chapter 35

Preparing to open …

Kate stood outside on the curb and looked up at the paint job on the repair from the fire. The late September blue sky was punctuated by a brilliant sun. A pleasant breeze blew around her and into the windows of her house. After all the renovation and the fire, Kate's Bed & Breakfast was finally ready to open just in time for the annual Adams fall festivities. The inn was booked solid every weekend for the events through Halloween. And why not? Anyone who wanted a proper Halloween fright came to Adams each weekend in October for the Bell Witch Festival for storytelling, the play *Spirit*, and the added traditional Halloween festivities for two days the weekend before Halloween.

The timer on her cellphone went off, and she hurried into the house to take her pumpkin-shaped orange sugar cookies out of the oven. She slid the parchment paper onto the wire racks and slid another batch onto the pan and into the oven. The new dishwasher chugged away next to the sink. Kate set the timer again then looked out the back door to the garage.

She hurried down the steps to the garden, such as it was, and walked to the garage. She opened the door and caught Will on the phone, lounging with his feet on his desk. Her car had been relegated to the driveway when Will had started his civil engineering business. It only made sense that he use the available space at the house. She owed him a fortune, but he just hushed her and kissed her whenever she asked him about it.

Kate checked the timer and then sat in a chair across from Will while he finished his call. When he hung up, she came around the desk and plopped into his lap.

"What can I do for you?" He wrapped his arms around her waist. "You smell like vanilla and sugar. Cookies?"

"Yes, I only have four more minutes to go grab the next tray from the oven." She wrapped her arms around his neck. "I just wanted to see you."

"And that is the brilliance of using the garage for my office, for the time being anyway. We'll need heat and A/C out here soon though."

"You know, we could convert this space into a bungalow and either use it as a short-term rental or move out here after we're married."

A woof answered her from beneath the desk.

"Beebe! So, that's where you got off to!" Kate checked her phone. "Gotta go! Don't need any burnt pumpkins."

He held fast to her for just a second longer. She kissed him then made her escape back to the kitchen.

Once Kate placed the last tray of cookies into the oven, she checked the dining table. Twelve place settings of sterling silver, crystal, and china were laid on her grandmother's lace tablecloth. A second table held her mother's lace tablecloth with her silverware, crystal plates, and goblets. Place cards were set at each chair. So many people had helped prepare the house to open for the fall season. This dinner was an act of appreciation. Satisfied that the tables were ready for guests, Kate returned to the kitchen to rescue the last batch of cookies.

In a second oven, a turkey roasted, stuffed with her favorite stuffing mix. Frozen cherry salad was ready. She popped two green bean casseroles into the oven. Everything would be ready in an hour, just when the guests were due to arrive.

The kitchen door to the garden opened admitting Beebe at a tear followed by Will.

"Anything I can do to help?" He snared her into a hug. "It smells so good in here."

Kate smiled and kissed him. "Everything will be ready as our guests arrive."

"Now's a good time to go home and get spiffed up?" Will kissed her back.

Kate nodded. "I need to change as well."

"But I like you just the way you are, Katie-girl." He smiled, and his eyebrows danced.

Kate laughed at his familiar rejoinder. "You're already pretty spiffy yourself."

Will kissed her and headed toward the front door. "I'll probably come with my parents to reduce the guest parking footprint out front."

"Sounds good. Hurry back."

Once Will closed the front door, Kate locked the kitchen door and double checked that Will had locked the front door. After all the random people who had entered the house over the summer, Kate was a little paranoid about someone entering the house, especially when she was changing or in bed.

Beebe met her on the stairs as she went to freshen up and change her clothes.

Kate was pulling the turkey from the oven when Will arrived with Maddy and Porter.

"Let me help with that." Will jumped into action taking the mitts from the counter and taking the hot pan from her. "Where am I going with it?"

Kate indicated the counter where a folded kitchen towel lay prepared to receive the hot pan.

Will quickly landed the bird on the towel. "Wow! It smells fantastic. Just like Thanksgiving."

"I thought that was appropriate for thanking all of our guests for their help in renovating and repairing the house."

Kate curled back the aluminum foil. A perfectly browned turkey was revealed with stuffing spilling into the pan.

"My mouth is watering."

Maddy and Porter wandered into the kitchen.

"It smells amazing in here." Porter reached into the pan and snagged a piece of dressing.

Maddy smacked his hand. "Don't be sampling here. This is not our kitchen."

Kate giggled. "Here, take these plates of cookies and scatter them around, so people feel free to take a cookie."

Porter took a plate and a cookie from it. "These look good enough to eat."

"I can't take you nowhere, can I?" Maddy took the

plate from him and a second plate into the dining room.

Porter took a bite of his cookie. "This cookie tastes great, Katie."

More guests arrived, and Will played host while Kate carved the turkey and loaded two platters, one for each table. A timer reminded her to remove the two green bean casseroles from the oven. Two vegetable trays came out of the refrigerator. She placed the food on a sideboard for buffet style serving.

Once all the guests had arrived, Kate rang a small dinner bell to get their attention. "Thanks to the hard work of all of you, this weekend we will have our first guests for the Red River storytelling. Will and I thank you. Will, lead us in prayer."

"Lord Heavenly Father, we thank you for the bounty we're about to receive. Bless the hands of our capable hostess. Bless the Bed & Breakfast and all those who will receive hospitality here. Bless the gathered friends who helped Katie's dream come true. Amen."

Once people began serving their plates, Kate went back to the kitchen and opened the butler's pantry. She brought out the multilayered cake she'd baked and decorated. She took it into the dining room and set it on a small table. Cake plates from both sets of place settings were stacked alternating. Cake forks and fall napkins sat beside the cake.

"Ooh!" Joe's voice sounded over the conversational tone. "Now, that's a cake."

All the guests looked at Kate and the cake. Appreciative sounds reverberated around the room.

"Guess I should save room for dessert!" Porter called out over the crowd.

Everyone laughed and continued filling their plates.

When it came time for cake, Will took the iced tea pitcher around to top off everyone's glasses.

Kate stood by the cake and raised her glass. "To all of you who have made my dream come true. Thank you for welcoming me into your community. We have navigated through some difficult challenges. All your hard work has made this house all I had wanted it to be. Thank you to all of you. Cheers!"

Glasses clinked.

Will joined her at the cake table. "Is this practice for our wedding cake?"

Kate jabbed him in the ribs. "Maybe. Let's get this place up and running before we solidify those plans."

Guests began tapping their glasses with their forks. "Kiss! Kiss!"

Will raised an eyebrow.

Kate smiled.

He took her in his arms and dipped her into a swoon-worthy kiss. Their guests, their friends, cheered.

Kate closed her eyes and whispered into Will's ear. "I want to remember this always, for the rest of our lives."

"Together." He kissed her cheek, eliciting more cheers.

Kate cut the cake, and Will served it.

About the Author

Diane E. Tatum began writing in grade school with short mystery stories, a play performed by her sixth-grade class, and a dictionary of supernatural beings. High school found her writing serial fiction with her friends, including developing characters and plot lines through hand-written notes.

Her first book, *Gold Earrings,* is an outgrowth of a short story written in a high school creative writing class. She is writing a historical Christian series called *Colonial Dream*. The first novel is *A Time to Fight*, the second is *A Time to Love*, and the third is *A Time to Choose*. She has also written a series of mysteries called *Mainstreet Mysteries: #1 Kudzu Sculptures, #2 Gemini Conspiracy, #3 Attic Visitation, #4 DNA Secrets, and #5 The Disappearing Diaspora*. The other novels are listed below.

In addition to her writing career, Diane taught middle school language arts for 11 years. She has worked as a church youth group leader and worker since 1981. She also served as an adjunct professor of English at Motlow State Community College.

She is loved and supported by her husband, Ken, and their two sons and daughters-in-law. Their four young grandsons are a joy to them all. Diane and Ken have a rescued racing greyhound Iggy who adds excitement at their house.

Books by Diane E. Tatum
Gold Earrings
Mission Mesquite
Oxford Fairy Tale
Colonial Dream, Book 1: A Time to Fight
Colonial Dream, Book 2: A Time to Love
Colonial Dream, Book 3: A Time to Choose
Main Street Mysteries #1: Kudzu Sculptures
Main Street Mysteries #2: The Gemini Conspiracy
Main Street Mysteries #3: Attic Visitations
Main Street Mysteries #4: DNA Secrets
Mainstreet Mysteries #5: Disappearing Diaspora
MISStletoe Romances: Dreaming of a Wedded Christmas
Nevermind Time: Cecilia's Y2 Key
Unordinary Romance: Finding Love in the Fog of

Aphasia
    Summer Secrets: Hiding in the Highlands
    Mysteries at Kate's B&B, Book 1: Surviving Renovation

    Coming soon!
    Colonial Dream, Book 4: A Time to Create
    Mysteries at Kate's B&B, Book 2: Trauma at the Fall Festival

257

Mysteries at Kate's B&B, Book 2: Trauma at the Fall Festival

Chapter 1
The first day …

October. Guests arrive today. Kate Winslow's first thoughts when the alarm kicked off. Beebe, her white lab puppy, cried out until she turned the sound off. She was groggy. Today was the first day of the business operations of Kate's Bed and Breakfast, and she'd slept poorly. She'd pay for that by mid-day. Meanwhile, Kate had much to do before three o'clock when the first guests were set to arrive.

She rolled out of bed and released Beebe from his crate. He was on the bed in seconds begging for hugs and rubs. Kate laughed at him and pulled the dog into her arms. He was Will's gift to her when he had also presented her with an engagement ring. Her hand felt empty without her ring which had been damaged in a fire. Will was handling the repair, so she tried not to think about it.

As Kate stepped out of the shower, she heard the front door slam followed by the beeping of the security code.

"Is that you, Will?" She pulled the towel tighter around her. Renovating the house had been fraught with crazy events no one could have expected.

"Yes, Sweetheart. I thought I'd get an early start."

His deep voice made her smile and sent shivers

through her. "Start the coffeemaker and the oven. I'll pop in the coffeecake after I throw on clothes."

"If we were married, I'd have already been here."

Was it her fault that they had committed to get the B&B up and running before planning a wedding? Maybe it was, but it didn't hurt to enjoy the engagement a little longer. The repair of her diamond ring was also something to consider.

Kate put on a pair of culottes and a crisp no sleeve shirt. Just because it was October didn't mean the weather would chill down with the flip of the calendar. She plucked a cardigan from the closet, just in case.

Beebe exploded from the bedroom as soon as Kate opened the door. He loved Will, and the dog was no doubt on a search for him. Kate walked down the carpeted stairs with the brass rug holders noting every squeak and creak. She still felt the presence of her Great-Aunt Katharine and her mom in the house she had inherited. The wood banisters and steps gleamed with polish. The house was ready. Was she?

Will appeared at the bottom of the steps holding a squirming Beebe.

"I see he found you." Kate smiled and hurried down the last stairs.

By the time she reached the bottom step, Will had set down Beebe and opened his arms to embrace her. Kate's arms wrapped about his neck.

"Good morning, Sweetheart." A kiss ensued while Beebe whined for more attention. Will whisked Kate from the bottom step and gently placed her on the floor. "I love you, Katie. It's a big day."

"I know. I'm nervous. What if I don't like them? What if they're scary?"

"Then I'll stay on the property in the garage/office, so I can help if things go sideways."

Kate shook her head. "I slept on that old sleeper sofa when I was here as a child. It wasn't all that comfortable then. I doubt it's gotten any better."

"That explains why it feels like home. I'm smelling you as a child after our many adventures." Will grinned. "Didn't you say you had a coffeecake to warm up?"

Kate escaped his comforting arms and headed toward the kitchen. Will followed after her grabbing her again around her waist. The coffee smelled delightful.

After breakfast, Will headed back to the garage/office. Kate went from bedroom to bedroom to ensure everything was ready for her weekend guests. She straightened bedspreads, checked towels, and made sure the hidden passageway doors were firmly in place to avoid losing anyone in the middle of the house. She planned to keep the hidden corridors a secret to her guests.

The phone ringing drew her back to the kitchen where she'd left her cell phone.

"Kate's B&B. This is Kate." She dropped into a chair at the breakfast table.

"Hi, Kate. This is Robert Guyten. We have reservations for this weekend."

"Yes, Mr. Guyten. I'm looking forward to your family's arrival this afternoon. Is everything all right?"

"We could be running late, Kate. We had a car problem. Is it okay if we arrive after six o'clock?"

Kate could hear shouting in the background, but that probably wasn't her business. "That would be fine.

Please arrive before eight. Once it's dark, I'd prefer to have guests registered with their own key, so I can lock the front door."

"That makes a lot of sense, Kate. We'll be sure to do that. Otherwise, I'll call and let you know."

Kate frowned. Her first paying customer seemed a little off, but maybe it was just a bad day for him. She shrugged and put the phone in her pocket. While she was at her Victorian reception desk, she put together her guests' activity packet: The Bell Witch Cave and Red River rafting on Saturday, tickets for the storytelling on Sunday, and Adams Station Barbeque and Trattoria Pizza gift cards. She stashed the envelopes in the slots and laid out four keys for the rooms and the front door. The Guytens were also bringing their two teenage girls. Kate had been assured the girls were mild-mannered and would present no problems.

Will burst in the kitchen door. Kate startled, then Beebe started barking, dashing down the stairs, and sliding into Will.

"What's going on?" Kate ran to him and hugged him. "Is everything okay?"

"Yes, it's great news!" Will hugged her and kissed her. "I have my first paying contract!"

Kate sighed. "That's fantastic. I was afraid something horrible had happened."

"No, no, no. Everything is fine. Better than fine. My business is taking off."

"That's great. With our summer's run of bad luck and with today being the first day of customers, I figured something horrible had happened. What's the contract for?"

Will's eyes brightened. "It's site preparation for a restaurant between Adams and Springfield. If they like what I do, I could get more of the construction planning contract."

Kate caught his excitement. "Congrats, Will! When do you start?"

"I'm headed out to the site now. I'll bring back lunch." He kissed her, petted the dog, and hurried out the front door.

As Kate watched Will cross the front porch, Sarah from church was walking up the steps with a large box. Will took the box from her and carried it into the house.

"He's helpful, isn't he?" Sarah came in after Will left.

"He's amazing, Sarah. What's in the box?" Kate carried it back to the kitchen table.

"Goodies for your guests that you won't have to make yourself. Rolls, bread, and croissants."

When Kate opened the box, the aroma of fresh yeasty bread escaped. "Oh, my! It smells delicious. If you could bottle this aroma, you could sell it to Realtors and kitchen designers. It could even be perfume! Thank you so much. Coffee?"

"Absolutely. My sister is watching the bakery while I run stuff around town."

"How much do I owe you for the baked goods?" Kate poured coffee into mugs, finishing the pot.

"Nothing this time. We can negotiate next time." Sarah dumped sugar and half 'n' half into her mug. "I think you and I could be great friends as well as business partners."

"I'd like that."

The day flew by until three. Kate watched the clock waiting for the Guytens to appear after then. Will brought a pizza to the house for them to share. By six, she was nervous they wouldn't show. By eight, she locked the front door and tried their number.

"Hello, Kate. I know I said we'd be there by eight, but the traffic in Nashville is bad due to a semi-truck turnover and fire. We're on our way. Don't give our beds away."

She could hear fighting in the background as well as an emergency siren. "There's nothing to be done about it. I'll wait up for you."

Will put his arm around her. "When do they plan to be here?"

"Don't know. There's a big traffic jam in Nashville with an overturned semi." Kate shivered. "This is making me nervous."

"I'll sleep in the garage tonight. Or I can sleep on the settee in the parlor." Will shrugged. "I'd feel better being on the premises when they arrive. C'mon, let's go sit in the swing."

Will made sure the kitchen door was closed and locked. They unlocked the front door and went out to the porch swing. Will rocked it gently with his foot with his arm around Kate. Crickets and tree frogs sang their night songs. She became sleepy.

Kate jerked awake when headlights washed across the front of the house.

Will roused at her startle. "Are they here?" He sounded sleepy. He pulled his phone from his pocket. "Ten forty-five? Katie, you need to institute a late fee. These folks have taken advantage of you."

Car doors slammed. Voices echoed in the dark. "Take your suitcase and backpack, Ellen. Sue, grab your pillows and your backpack." Luggage wheels wobbled on the concrete front walk. Four people appeared eventually in the porchlight. Mr. Guyten must have been six foot five inches tall. Two lanky girls, twins in name only, were opposites – one had black hair and wore all black including black lipstick while the other was fair and blonde in summer white clothing. Bringing up the rear was a mousy Mrs. Guyten. Her arms were full of luggage, pillows, and tote bags.

Will hurried down the walk to take some of the load from Mrs. Guyten.

"Welcome to Kate's B&B. I'm Kate, your hostess for your stay during the Bell Witch Fall Festival."

"Cool." The twin in black gave her a hand signal Kate didn't know.

The girls tromped onto the porch and filed into the house.

"Sorry we're so late. Couldn't be helped, I guess." Mr. Guyten held out his hand to Will. "I'm Robert Guyten. She's Kate. Who are you, sir?"

"Will Bell. Kate's fiancée." Will shook Mr. Guyten's hand.

"Please come in." Kate reached Mrs. Guyten and walked up the steps with her. The mom looked exhausted. Kate's heart went out to her. The family failed to help Mom Guyten with their belongings. Mr. Guyten seemed to believe Will was in charge which made Kate furious.

Kate took her place behind the reception desk and sorted through the materials for the weekend and their keys. The girls were sharing one room next to their parents. Kate had them around the hallway from her bedroom. That gave Kate privacy from the family.

"Tomorrow, you have tickets to the Bell Witch Cave and the Red River Rafting experience. The storytelling Red River Tales is Sunday afternoon. You each have a room key and the key to the front door. You have gift cards for two local eateries. Breakfast is at eight."

"Eight o'clock, Mom! It's nearly midnight now. I'm sleeping. No way am I getting up for eight o'clock breakfast." The twin in black stomped her foot and crossed her arms.

"If Ellen doesn't have to eat breakfast, I don't want to either. This whole trip is ridiculous." The twin in white agreed with her sister.

"Come on, girls, let's get some sleep. We'll all feel better in the morning." Robert rounded the teenagers up and herded them up the stairs.

"I'm Margie." Mom Guyten held out a hand to Kate. "I'm sorry we're late. I look forward to the breakfast you have planned. Thank you for waiting up for us."

Kate took her hand and pulled her into a hug. "Please sleep well. I'll see you in the morning."

Margie nodded. A tear slid down her cheek. Then Will went with her up the stairs with the luggage the rest of the family had conveniently forgotten.

Kate turned out the lights in the kitchen and made sure the nightlights were on in the halls and steps. She locked the front door and turned around into Will's chest.

"Ah!" Kate grasped his shoulders. "You scared me."

"Exactly. Give me the key to the bedroom nearest you. No way am I letting the Addams family be here with only you."

Kate reached in the drawer and handed him the key to room #2. "Thank you. Be sure to let your mom know what you're doing."

"Already sent her a text." Will grinned and hugged her. "Come on. You and I are fixing breakfast in the morning."

For more info about the Bell Witch:

The story of the Bell Witch is taught as part of Tennessee History in 7th grade. John Bell's death is the only investigated and authenticated death caused by an evil spirit in the U.S.

Bell, Charles Bailey, A Descendant. *The Bell Witch of Tennessee* (the black book). 1934.

Ingram, M. V. *Authenticated History of The Bell Witch and Other Stories of the World's Greatest Unexplained Phenomenon* (the red book), including "Our Family's Trouble" by Drewry Bell. 1894.

"The Bell Witch Cave." *Ghost Adventures* Season 13 Episode 5, (This seems to change seasons and episodes).

Websites: www.bellwitchcave.com/
https://adamstennessee.net/community/businesses/

www.ingramcontent.com/pod-product-compliance
Lightning Source LLC
Chambersburg PA
CBHW060912210726
48293CB00006B/2063